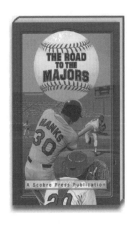  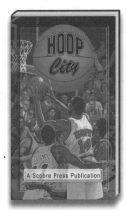

On the back of this page is an order form for the following three Scobre titles. Each book is $9.95 plus $2.00 shipping and handling. (Shipping is waived on purchases of two or more books.) If you would like to purchase one or more Scobre books, please fill out, detach, and mail in this order form with appropriate payment to:

Scobre Press Corporation
2255 Calle Clara
La Jolla, CA 92037

SCOBRE PRESS

"The athletes behind the action...."

To purchase copies of *The Road to the Majors, Hoop City,* or *Keeper* please fill out, detach, and send in the form below. Send checks payable to Scobre Press.
MAIL TO: Scobre Press, 2255 Calle Clara, La Jolla, CA 92037

QUANTITY	TITLE	PRICE
	THE ROAD TO THE MAJORS	
	HOOP CITY	
	KEEPER	
		TOTAL

SHIP TO:

NAME:

ADDRESS:

CITY/STATE: ZIP:

To pay by credit card, purchase at **www.scobre.com**

Baseball...

...what
dreams
are
made of.

4

San Diego®

Let the
dreams begin.

COX.
COMMUNICATIONS

KiDS

FOUNDATION

To the Children:

Reading fosters a love of learning that lasts a lifetime. Numerous studies show that students who read outside of school do better in school and that access to books and other interesting reading materials is directly related to student achievement. San Diego READS supports you in your efforts to read and achieve.

DON'T QUIT

When things go wrong, as they sometimes will,
When the road you're trudging seems all uphill,
When the funds are low, and the debts are high,
And you want to smile, but you frown a bit,
Rest if you must, but don't you quit.

Life is strange with its twists and turns,
As everyone of us sometimes learns,
And many a failure turns about,
When he might have won had he stuck it out;
Don't give up though the pace seems slow,
You may succeed with another blow.

Success is failure turned inside out,
The silver tint of the clouds of doubt,
And you can never tell how close you are,
It may be near when it seems so far;
So stick to the fight when you're hardest hit,
It's when things seem worst
That you must not quit.

Author Unknown

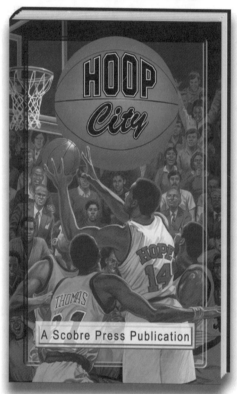

THE ROAD TO THE MAJORS

BY

SCOTT BLUMENTHAL
AND
BRETT HODUS

www.scobre.com

Scobre Press Corporation
2255 Calle Clara
La Jolla, CA 92307

Scobre Press books may be purchased for educa-
tional, business or sales promotional use.

Second Scobre edition published 2002.

Edited by Debra Ginsberg
Illustrated by Larry Salk
Cover Design by Michael Lynch

ISBN 0-9708992-0-3

www.scobre.com

To all the dreamers...

We at Scobre Press are proud to bring you the first book in what will be a series of such stories. The goal of Scobre is to influence young people by entertaining them with books about athletes who act as role models. The moral dilemmas facing the athletes in a Scobre story run parallel to situations facing many young people today. After reading a Scobre book, our hope is that young people will be able to respond to adversity in their lives in the same heroic fashion as the athletes depicted in our books.

This book is about Jimmy Hanks, a fictional baseball player. To us and to everyone who reads this book, Jimmy is much more than just a "made-up" ballplayer, he is an example of what it is to dream big dreams and to fight every day to make those dreams a reality. His story of perseverance, determination, and belief in himself is one we all could learn from.

We invite you now to come along with us, sit down, get comfortable, and read a book that will dare you to dream big dreams as well. Scobre dedicates this book to all the people who are chasing their own dreams. We hope that Jimmy inspires you to reach for the stars.

Here's Jimmy Hanks, and his "Road to the Majors."

Chapter 1: "Up, Down, or Out?"

I ran in place, kicking up small chunks of dirt from beneath the grass like a human lawn mower. I wanted to keep my feet moving to fight the morning chill of central Florida. I couldn't play with frozen feet, not today. I looked down at my beat up size twelve cleats. They looked especially worn out next to the bright green grass of the baseball diamond and the true brown of the infield dirt. I promised myself that if I made the jump to Double-A ball, I'd buy a new pair. That morning, I would find out whether or not I'd be able to afford them.

"Assignment day" is the day that each player is assigned to a particular Minor League team, or told to go straight home. I'd been awake since 5:00 a.m. that morning, wondering where I would be playing in the upcoming season. Every year, three days before spring training ends, Minor Leaguers around the country can count on the most nerve-racking day of their season. Today was that day.

Cold sweat dripped from my forehead onto the soft green grass of Kissimmee, Florida. I was twenty-four years old and if I wanted to have a legitimate chance of playing Major League Baseball, I couldn't spend another season in Single-A. This spring training marked the start of my second full season in the Minor Leagues. I had to keep moving up. If I stood still for too long, I would need to find a new profession. I ran in place faster, kicking up bigger and bigger chunks of dirt. I was excited. In a few hours, I would find out my baseball destiny.

I started the day by working on my defense. Coach

Benny Catta, my manager during my season in Single-A, pounded grounders to me at third base. The first ball he hit shot off his bat like a rocket. I tried to locate the dirty brown thing as it cut through the 7:00 a.m. fog. Usually, I'd field the ball cleanly, but this one took a strange hop that only a baseball could take. The grounder hit the edge of the freshly cut grass, and changed direction like a pinball. I reacted and dove to my left, trying to save myself from the embarrassment of an empty mitt. I missed. The ball slipped away from me like a pretty girl on a passing bus. And in those moments, I could really feel what baseball was all about. The game had taught me how to overcome failure. I stood up and brushed myself off, ready to dive again.

I pulled my hat down hard on my head, trying to hide inside for a moment or two. Then I punched the center of my mitt. This punch was a signal to myself. "Wake up Jimmy, make this practice count." The glove I wore on my hand had spent more than a few nights carefully wrapped in rubber bands beneath my pillow. I'd had that mitt since high school. I punched the leather again as I watched a few of the guys arrive for the long day ahead. I knew how much this day would mean to my life as a baseball player, and to the lives of all the ballplayers who sweated for weeks during spring training in Kissimmee. I could see by their nervous looks that they'd marked "assignment day" on their calendars as well. We all fought and bled for one chance to play the game we loved at the highest level. Getting there was the hard part.

The road to the Majors is hardly a smooth ride. To become a Major Leaguer a player must first survive Minor League Baseball, the training ground where potential Major Leaguers are plucked like apples from a tree. Only the very best apples have any chance at reaching the 'big leagues.' But first, these exceptional players must pass through six grueling levels of competitive baseball.

In the Minor Leagues, we traveled for hours at a time on packed buses that smelled like high school gym class. We slept in hotel rooms that Major Leaguers would use as closets. We lived out of suitcases for months at a time, never knowing when we would be moved up, down, or out of the system. While Major Leaguers played in big cities like Los Angeles and New York, we endured six-hour rain delays in Shreveport and double headers in Erie. We played through injuries, and dove onto unkempt fields countless times with little chance of making a play, and we did all of this every day. But in the end, we were faced with the harsh reality that while some of us would get to the Majors, most of us would not.

I fielded a few more grounders from Benny and fired the ball across the diamond to first base. Nick Erickson stood waiting with his glove extended, ready to receive my next throw. He yelled at me, "Hey! Don't pull me off the bag this time. I don't know what I'm doing out here." Nick was a great outfielder, but he was defi-nitely not a first baseman. I guess I didn't listen to him, because I made us both look bad on the next throw. The ball bounced in front of Nick and skipped into his leg. He laughed sarcastically, "Nice throw Jimmy. You trying to kill me?"

I laughed along with him, "Well, you're still on the bag. You told me not to pull you off the bag, you didn't say I couldn't hit ya."

Nick laughed harder. We could never stay angry with each other, we'd been friends forever.

A few seconds later, a commanding voice rang out from behind me. "Balance yourself before you make that throw, Hanks." I turned around and saw Bill Putnam, a coach in the Dallas Lonestars organization, and he wasn't laughing. The smile quickly disappeared from my face. I should have known that someone was watching. Someone was always watching. The Dallas Lonestars are a Major League franchise and they wouldn't leave anything to chance. During our time in Florida, we were observed closely by the coaches and executives in the Lonestars system that assigned us to our particular teams. Every year Dallas drafts fifty players, and more than half will play Minor League Baseball. For every player who enters the six-team farm system, a player must exit. It's a numbers game and it doesn't benefit slow learners. I knew this. I punched my mitt again, this time much harder. "Buck up, Jimmy, big day for you." My palms began to sweat, and although I knew I had done everything in my power to leave a positive impression on my bosses, I was still nervous. I think everybody was. After all, we were just boys chasing the same dream.

A few minutes later Benny had finished hitting grounders to me. I walked over to Nick at first base and patted him on the back, "Sorry about that throw, you all right?" I felt bad about hitting him.

"Yeah, I'm fine." Nick and I looked over at our teammates who had begun stretching and warming up. I wondered who among these guys would be around tomorrow, and who would be going home today. Nick continued, "So, what do you think about today?"

I knew exactly what he was talking about, "Double-A, I hope. You?"

As usual, Nick had a great answer on the tip of his tongue, "I'm hoping to go right to the show." The 'show' was the Major Leagues, and we both laughed, knowing that neither one of us had a shot at that yet. The thought of playing in the Majors sounded great, but our next step was advancing beyond Single-A.

The early morning "stretch and catch" was how we loosened up our legs and arms for the long day ahead. Usually, this was a time filled with chatter between the guys where we heard stories from the previous night's adventures. We talked about sports and the upcoming baseball season. Everybody had his favorite team, and his favorite player, and we'd argue back and forth just like we were kids. These guys were from a hundred different towns and cities, and their stories were as different as their backgrounds. The chatter was friendly, never too personal, and almost always a welcomed distraction. And although the friendships were real, so was the competition. The guy who slept with his head leaned against your shoulder on a seven-hour bus ride to nowhere, could be the same guy who took your position at the next level.

This was the reason that the normal chatter ceased on "assignment day." Today it was too personal. This was a day that we all dreaded, if not for ourselves, then for the guy whose position we would steal at the next level.

The boys lined up across from each other in the outfield, and threw the ball back and forth like we'd done a thousand times. I played catch with Chad Barnett, my teammate from Single-A ball. At six feet tall and two hundred pounds, Chad was a guy who just looked like a ballplayer.

As the early morning fog crept away from us, everything and everyone became silent. The only sound that could be heard was the popping of the mitts, as the baseball snapped back and forth between partners. A rhythm developed. Somebody coughed, "pop," a bird flew over head, "pop," Chad threw a laser that smacked the palm of my glove, "pop." Then, as if from nowhere, a voice said, "Bobby Ashbury, you're first, come with me to the clubhouse." The silence was broken. Bobby was the first person to find out where he would be playing next season. Everyone immediately came to attention. Each player was now aware that the next person to be summoned to the clubhouse could be him. For some guys, "assignment day" would mark the end of their baseball careers, for others, just the beginning.

I recognized the voice that broke the morning silence. Jerry Retskin's strong Southern twang always got my attention. Jerry and his crew evaluated Minor Leaguer on top of Minor Leaguer. They had a wealth of knowledge and experience about what type of player and person would be a Major Leaguer and what type would not. We all played "catch" together and awaited the judgement of Jerry and his partner, Phil Toombs. The two of them made the final decision as to which of the six Lonestar Minor League teams we would play on, if we made a team at all. I was waiting for my turn in their office. I believed that I had progressed, and I prayed that Jerry and Phil had noticed. But I wouldn't find out until I met with them in the clubhouse, located just beyond the wall in left field.

There is rarely any expression on a player's face when he returns from the clubhouse. Baseball etiquette strictly forbids gloating, and teaches a player to be humble as well. One by one players exited the clubhouse and quietly told their closest friends if they'd been moved up, down, or out of the system. Some guys just got back into line and kept throwing, seemingly unaffected. The last thing anyone wanted to do was rub their promotion into somebody else's face, or put their head in their hands and cry, showing how their demotion had broken them. But deep inside, beyond the diamond and the glove and the stirrup socks, guys do cry when they're released. Those tears drop later, when you pack up your stuff, the same stuff you packed on road trip after road trip, only this time you pack for home. The trip is over and you leave the clubhouse one last time to embark on the rest of your life - - without baseball.

I toweled off after another run through the morning obstacle course. I didn't understand why we had to run the course three times, but I never questioned a coach's decision. I noticed Chad Barnett walking back from the clubhouse. He moved slowly but with confidence, chin up, his face stolid and expressionless. I wanted to ask him where he was playing, what had happened, what did Jerry say to you, did he tell you the news right away? I had a million more of these questions, but kept them to myself. I couldn't find any words and ended up saying, "Hey buddy." The comment seemed idiotic, but it turned out to be strangely appropriate.

Chad responded, "Hey Jim." He let out a small giggle, without showing his teeth. I felt a great sense of relief, guessing that his laughter signified some decent news.

"So, uh, where are you playing?" I quietly asked him, trying not to pressure him.

Chad spoke through a tight grin that concealed his obvious excitement. "Amarillo, Double-A ball, Jimbo."

I sighed with relief. "Congratulations, Chad. That's really awesome," Chad and I touched fists, a gesture of congratulations that has replaced the high five in dugouts everywhere. He looked as if he was about to say something, but he didn't. I understood. There was nothing to say. If I was joining him in Texas, we'd celebrate tonight, and if I wasn't, we'd probably never see each other again. There was more than just baseball on the line that day. Our friendship was also at stake.

I bent down to tie the shoelace that had come undone someplace between the obstacle course and my conversation with Chad. When I picked my head back up, the sun was glaring into my eyes and I could barely make out the figure of Brian Peterson, another Major League hopeful. He looked rattled.

"Jimmy, you're up. Hope someone around here gets some good news," Brian spoke softly and made sure to avoid my eyes. I untied, and then tied my other shoelace slowly and deliberately, avoiding the panicked look I had seen on Brian's face a moment earlier. I was sure he'd be packing his things for home.

I made my way toward the locker room as quickly as possible. I wanted to get this over with. When I reached the door to Jerry's office, I paused before entering and took a deep breath. I turned the doorknob and went into the room. The office was poorly lit. A flickering Dallas Lonestars lamp sat on the corner of the desk, but other than that, the place was bare.

Jerry and Phil welcomed me into the office and made me feel comfortable. I had a friendly, yet professional, relationship with both of them. "How's it going guys?" I asked them as I shook their hands before taking a seat across from them in a chair that didn't look strong enough to hold me. They knew me as a laid back California kid. And even then, I did my best to keep my composure and lean back in the chair.

Phil finally answered my question, "We're doing fine, Jim. Thanks for asking." He was all business today. He reached across his desk and fiddled with the light bulb inside of the Lonestars lamp. The room became bright. "Well, I guess we can begin by telling you that you are now a member of the Amarillo Dusters."

In one simple sentence I had received my promotion from Single-A Kissimmee to Double-A Amarillo. I breathed a sigh of relief as softly as I could, and I think that Phil noticed because he smiled. I smiled back. After only one season at the Single-A level, I was moving up.

I was through leaning back in my chair at this point. Jerry broke in with his southern accent, "Congratulations on that accomplishment. And I know it's not your style, but you can give yourself a quick pat on the back if you'd like, 'cause the jump from A ball to Double-A is a real important one." I was excited and relieved. Double-A ball sure sounded sweet, but I wasn't going to pat myself on the back until I was standing on a Major League field.

I was speechless. I shook their hands and I don't know if I walked, jumped, or floated right out of the clubhouse. I was going to Double-A Amarillo! I was moving to Texas. I was now only two steps away from playing in the Major Leagues. I was closing in on my dream faster than I had expected. I was hitting and fielding better than ever. Life was great.

All of those extra ground balls at third base and the extra batting practice had paid off.

"Jimmy Hanks, playing third base for the Amarillo Dusters." That sure had a nice ring to it.

Practice had come to a close. I was showered, dressed, and out of the clubhouse before half the guys had even left the field. On the way to my car I stopped at the pay phone to call my parents. I was so excited that I dialed the wrong number twice before I punched in the number I'd known by heart for years. Mom screamed when I told her the news. I hung up the telephone feeling great.

Hector Gomez was standing behind me, waiting for his chance to use the phone. "Hey Jimmy, congratulations, buddy." Hector and I had both been promoted to Amarillo. "Thanks, man," I said. "You too." We slapped hands and I gave him the telephone. "Hey Jim!" Hector shouted out to me just before I got into my car.

I rolled down the window. "What's up?" I said. Hector smiled, "Do you know where the heck Amarillo is?" I shrugged my shoulders and drove away. I had no idea where Amarillo was. I did know, however, that Amarillo meant I was one giant step closer to reaching my dream of playing Major League Baseball.

After practice, I drove back to the condominium that a few of my teammates and I were renting during spring training. On the short ride from the field, I smiled from ear to ear and blasted the radio. I can't remember what song was on, but I remember it fit my upbeat mood perfectly.

Shortly after I arrived at the condo, my friends and teammates joined me in our living room. We were all excited about what had happened that day, and the atmosphere was almost giddy. Everyone was laughing at stupid jokes, and we were all a little louder than usual. As it turned out, all five of us who'd rented the place had received promotions to Double-A. Kevin Cove, Chad Barnett, Nick Erickson, Leon Thompson and I readied ourselves for a night of celebration on the town. But first, we needed pizza. I took the initiative and grabbed the telephone.

"Get extra cheese on one of 'em Jimmy," Kevin Cove shouted as I dialed the number to Mama Mia's Pizza.

"Hello…yes, I'd like two large pizzas, one with pepperoni and one with extra cheese… Twenty minutes?…O.K., thanks."

I hung up the phone and flicked on the television set. I glanced around the room, and stared at everyone. This is what I always remember when I think about that night. The television, the excited faces, the conversations, the way the room was set up. The way Leon leaned back in the corner lounge chair. How Kevin and Chad argued over the remote control on the long green couch next to the window. I remembered Nick and I sitting on the adjacent couch that faced the front door, talking about the weather in Texas, the difference between Single-A and Double-A, and then nothing at all. There was no signal that something was terribly wrong. The doorbell rang.

"That was quick," Leon said from the corner. "Didn't you just hang up the phone about five minutes ago?"

I reached into my pocket for some money. "They say they have the fastest pizza delivery in town."

Chad Barnett chimed in, laughing, "Five minute delivery, what's this guy driving, a rocket?"

I got up from my seat and walked over to the door, still chuckling at Chad's comment. My mouth was starting to water for the pizza. If there was ever a night for a five-minute delivery, this was it. I went over to the door like someone might do a million times in their life. Never thinking about what's on the other side. I turned the doorknob without care, without fear, and without thought. A split second later the door slammed shut behind me, and two men holding handguns were standing in our living room.

"All of you get on the floor right now, this is a holdup!" One of them screamed. He was dressed in black and his face was hidden by a dark wool ski mask. I looked into his eyes and a chill shot down my spine. His partner was also dressed in black. A green bandana covered the bottom part of his face and another one covered the top portion. I could only see his eyes as well.

I immediately dropped to the floor, eager to comply with the men. We would put ourselves in much more danger if we didn't cooperate. I tried to put my arms in a position that

12

would look the least threatening. I didn't want either of them to think that I was going to try to be a hero. If money was all they wanted, that was not a problem. Their guns were what scared me.

"All right, where's the money?" the man with the ski mask asked gruffly. At once, all five of us began to answer, "In the drawers, in my pocket, in my soccer bag." The simultaneous blurting out of answers appeared to fluster the man in charge momentarily. "No, no - one at a time!" He spoke with force behind his words. He reached down and tapped me hard on the shoulder with his gun. "You first." I had only seen guns in the movies but I knew how dangerous they were. I spoke deliberately, making sure not to do anything that would make the man nervous or upset, "My money is in my old soccer bag, the blue one with the Tidal Waves logo on it. It's to my left on the floor." I looked out of the corner of my eye and pointed at the bag, making sure that "old trusty" was still there. It was there; it was always there. Ever since I was fourteen years old my soccer bag had never left my side.

I glanced closely at the word "Tidal Waves" on the side of the little blue bag. I began to remember why I had been carrying it around with me for such a long time. I thought about how much I cherished that bag. I'd kept that tired thing intact for almost a decade.

I stared at the man who pointed a gun at me. I searched for a trace of humanity in the dark abyss of his eyes. I looked for a human expression hidden behind his bandana. I listened to rough voices, and quickly glanced at scared faces all around the room. And then I was numb. I stared long and hard at the white writing on the bag that spelled out the word "Tidal Waves." And I remembered that before baseball, I was a soccer player...

Chapter 2: "A Tough Fall"

It's funny the things you remember at the strangest times in your life. Two men pointed loaded guns at my head and all I could picture was my mother, standing in our kitchen making peanut butter and jelly sandwiches. We lived in a suburb of San Diego. Dad worked close by, and we all loved the beach. So for us, there was no place like Oceantown, California.

"Jimmy, can you bring this up to your room? I don't want your smelly soccer bag sitting in my kitchen." She cut the sandwiches into triangles, and I poked my brother Dave, in his ribs, thinking my mother wouldn't see. "Now please." She always spoke in a pleasant tone yet her voice demanded immediate action. "And stop hitting your brother." Sometimes I felt like Mom's eyes were everywhere.

I jumped up from my seat and picked up my Tidal Waves bag from the floor. I ran up the stairs, throwing the bag into my room in the careless way that twelve year-olds throw things. A soccer ball rolled out onto the carpeted floor. I tapped it around with my feet a few times. I loved kicking that ball.

My mother's voice rang out from the bottom of the stairs, "Jimmy, lunch is ready. Stop kicking the ball in the house and come downstairs." I placed it back in the bag and walked down the stairs.

I always felt so comfortable kicking the soccer ball. I could imagine how Tiger Woods must have felt holding a golf club, walking to the local course after school. And Peyton

Manning had to feel like the football was made for his hand when he tossed it at the high school field, throwing perfect pass after perfect pass. And when Jeff Gordon got his driver's license, he must have thought that he owned the road. I had this kind of feeling every time I touched a soccer ball.

I was always decent at baseball and basketball, but soccer was my passion when I twelve years old. I remember I used to practice with Danny Stevenson, my best friend when I was a kid. One day, after school, we were kicking the ball around at the soccer field just up the street. Danny was his usual confident self and he ordered me to respect his powerful right foot. "Go back a few steps. Further. Move back like ten more feet, I want to really air this one out." Danny always spoke like he played, with tremendous enthusiasm. He was constantly challenging himself and his intensity motivated me to move faster on the field. I sprinted back to about thirty or forty yards away, and much to my surprise, he booted one over my head.

I frantically tried to run the ball down but during my dash, I tripped, and fell hard onto the grass.

"Jimmy? You O.K.?" Danny was concerned, but really he just wanted to kick the ball again. He approached me, realizing that I wasn't getting up right away. "Tough fall," Danny said. He chased down the soccer ball and began juggling it on his knee, impatient to get started again. I spoke, but was a little dazed. "What?" Danny repeated himself, still juggling, "Tough fall, you took a tough fall."

I looked at the grass stains on the front of the shirt that

I took so much pride in wearing. "My San Diego University shirt," I groaned, sliding my hand down my right shoulder and moving my fingers toward a hole in the fabric. I had ripped my favorite shirt.

I felt my bare skin through a large hole. I looked up at Danny and spoke as if I wanted him to do something, "I ripped my shirt." I was panicked. Danny thought he could solve my problem. "Don't worry, Jim, I've got an extra shirt." He ran to get his soccer bag, his intensity unfazed.

A few moments later, Danny was back, dribbling the ball in a zig-zag motion. My eyes were immediately drawn to his Tidal Waves bag and I completely forgot about my shirt. This was not the first time I had admired that bag. The strange light blue color and the huge wave that crashed over the words "BAYSIDE TIDAL WAVES" always mesmerized me. I wanted one of those bags. After seeing his bag, I was reminded of my quest to become a Tidal Wave. A tremendous sense of excitement pumped through my body. I stole the soccer ball from Danny and dribbled down toward a tree that we marked as the goal. He followed quickly, motivated by my sudden competitive urge. We raced for about fifty yards and I could feel him at my heels the entire time. I thought about the tryouts that would be taking place in just a few months. I knew I would need to get faster and stronger before those crucial days.

I was about ten yards from the tree when I thought I had enough separation for a shot. I swung my leg back, ready to fire. But an instant before I made contact, Danny slid in from behind me, knocking the ball away. When we rose to our

17

feet, he was the one dribbling. He reared back and shot a bullet that smacked the tree directly in the center. "Goal!" Danny shouted. I hung my head. I knew I had a lot more practicing to do before I would be a Tidal Wave.

"Nice play," I said without looking at him. I tried to catch my breath, but I was beaten. Danny sat down on the grass. I followed his lead, not wanting to sit before he did. "When are tryouts for the 'Waves again? I gotta make the team and get one of those bags." I always used to say this, even though I knew exactly when the tryouts were.

"I've told you like eight times, Jimbo. The tryouts are during baseball season, first week of April. And the answer is gonna be exactly the same when you ask me again tomorrow." He knew how much I wanted to play for the Tidal Waves.

The Tidal Waves were an elite group of soccer players from the San Diego area. I really wanted to be known as one of those guys but my age had held me back. While I was waiting for my thirteenth birthday, Danny was playing soccer for the 'Waves. In the upcoming year, I hoped to join him on the field.

The first week of April finally rolled around. Unfortunately, on the day of the tryouts, Danny and I had to go to baseball practice. My mind couldn't focus on baseball and I played terribly. We left practice early to ensure that we didn't miss the tryout, and were hazed appropriately by our teammates for our premature departure.

Doug Bird, a scrawny little guy with a big mouth, would not let me escape without getting in the last word.

"Oh, we see how it is, Jim, soccer is more important

than baseball. Fine, we don't need you anyway," he said sarcastically, laughing at his own joke. The rest of the guys joined Doug in laughter. He was right though, soccer was more important to me than baseball, especially on that day.

We arrived at the soccer field and stepped out of my mother's car without speaking. Danny and I walked onto the choppy grass slowly but steadily. There were hordes of guys trying out for the Tidal Waves, and they all looked bigger and stronger than me. Soon, we were immersed in the large crowd.

I noticed the field was in pretty poor shape, but I had grown accustomed to playing on such weathered fields. The torn up grass covered a bumpy ground that was peppered by small rocks. The lines designating out of bounds were faded, and the netting on the goals were tangled and torn.

I walked gingerly over to the sidelines, sitting down to put on my shin-guards and lace up my cleats. Danny sat down next to me. All of the other guys from last year's squad stood in a row, guarding their field like a gate. I hoped that none of the returning Tidal Waves had noticed me and I could just go about the business of playing soccer. I peered up and noticed that I was in the spotlight. All of the elder Tidal Waves were staring at me, knowing full well who I was. Obviously, Danny had told them about me. They stood together as protectors of their soccer field, and they looked like the most intimidating group I had ever seen. One of the bigger guys waved in my direction. I gave a small nod, thinking he might have been waving at me. I thought wrong. A moment later, Danny waved back to him and stood up, joining his teammates in line. He walked away and became one of them.

Shortly thereafter, Danny approached me from the line of Tidal Waves. He smiled, "How ya feeling?" I looked back at him and tried to sound composed. "I feel pretty good. I mean…great. I feel great." He looked unconvinced of this, and patted me on the back. "Don't worry so much. Come over with me and meet some of the guys. I think it's a good idea for you to get to know everyone before practice starts."

I thought that meeting the guys was a good idea as well, but my body didn't seem to agree. My throat had sunk into my stomach and speaking became an almost impossible task. I wanted to take a sip from my water bottle but feared I would spill on my shirt and look like a complete idiot. We walked towards the row of guys and Danny introduced me to them. There were seven returning Tidal Waves, leaving seven spots open to the rest of us that tried out.

I stood uncomfortably in front of the wall of guys as they judged me. I heard a few snickers, a few guys carried on with their conversations, and the rest of them just stared at me, blankly.

Danny introduced me to them. "Hey guys, this is my friend Jimmy from Oceantown. Let's make sure we get him the ball today, O.K?" Danny had spoken, but everyone just kept staring at me, nobody even acknowledged that he had said a word.

That is until a really big guy with short black whiskers extending from his chin and upper lip, chimed in, "From Oceantown, huh?"

I answered him quickly, trying to be friendly, "Yeah, I've-" He cut me off. "Are you a surfer?" I didn't want to answer this question, but I did anyway. "Sure, I surf, but I play soccer and base-" He cut me off again. "Yeah, you're definitely a surfer boy. You got that wavy hair and everything...dude." He tried to match the surfer lingo that he thought was prevalent in Oceantown.

Most of the guys who were on the team were from Bayside and they were not too fond of anyone who was not from their hometown. I was from Oceantown, which was regarded as a surfer's haven, so I already had one strike against me when dealing with these jocks. All of the guys, except Danny, started to laugh at me and my wavy hair. I knew that it was time to walk away. I was no longer nervous. I was determined. I would show them that the "surfer dude" could do more than just ride waves.

Practice began and we were each assigned to a team of seven players. I was positioned at left forward, although I am naturally a right forward. On the first exchange, the center on our team nudged me the ball. His kick hit the instep of my right foot and I pushed up the field as fast as I could. I dribbled to the outside and passed the first defender with ease. He was one of the guys on last year's squad, and I think my speed caught him off-guard. I still had two guys left to beat before I could line up a shot on goal.

I think that an athlete can sense a challenge when one is approaching. I could see that the two guys I had left to beat were no longer susceptible to a surprise attack, they were ready. I noticed that the goalie, who'd been standing idle until I reached about the forty-five-foot line, suddenly began to move around, bending his knees and spreading his arms wide. The first defender slid in front of me in an attempt to steal the ball. I was able to float a pass over his head, a trademark move of mine. The ball landed softly in front of me and I kept dribbling. Now I had everyone's attention. There was only one man left to beat before a showdown with the goalie.

The next defender was coming straight at me with reckless abandon. I touched the ball with the inside of my left cleat as he charged at me. After avoiding his slide, I was past him with the ball in front of my right foot. It was now me against the goalie. Instead of trying to fake him out with another fancy move, I decided to show off my power. This was a tryout and I had to show everything in my repertoire. I dribbled twice more and drilled a twenty-footer towards the left corner of the goal. My right-footed blast left the goalie frozen, and the ball bounced around in the back corner of the ragged net like a flopping fish.

I had scored on the first play of Tidal Waves tryouts. The "surfer dude" was flashing his soccer skills. But my excitement was short lived. "Hey, let's pass the ball out here. If I wanted to watch a highlight video, I would've had you guys send me tapes; now let's play as a team!" The deep and angry voice ended my victory parade. I looked toward the sideline and saw Coach Custis. He was exactly like Danny had advertised. He stood with hunched shoulders, and his shiny bald head was half-covered by a Tidal Waves hat that looked a few years old. I knew he was speaking directly to me because no one else had even touched the ball.

Coach Custis had scared me straight and I started passing every time I got my foot on the ball. Losing my confidence to create in the open field made me passive and the bigger guys were making me pay the price. On one particular play, I was dribbling toward midfield and a monstrous halfback came charging at me like a runaway train. I passed the ball off immediately, but his momentum carried him right through me. I took a heavy bump and was floored. I thought I'd broken my ribs.

Danny came over to help me, sensing that I'd been taken out of my game, "Jimmy, relax. Start playing man! Pretend that it's just me and you practicing out here." I thought about what he said. I remembered that I was actually good at this game. I jumped to my feet and got back into the flow. My confidence grew when I dropped a few nice passes onto my teammates who were able to kick them in for easy goals. The practice continued like that for a while and I picked up momentum with each play.

By the time practice had ended, I was completely exhausted. I collapsed onto the sidelines and took a few gulps from my water bottle. The big guy who'd hazed me about my hair before the tryouts called out to me as I unlaced my cleats. I didn't remember his name, and I remember feeling bad about that.

"You played good out there today," he said, "I think you have a real shot to make this team." When the day began I never imagined the team bully would be on my side. I was beginning to feel like a Tidal Wave.

That night I made lists of different players who could

be chosen for the Tidal Waves. Fourteen guys would make the team, and when I made my lists, I was never further down than eighth or ninth. I was confident that Coach Custis would have good news for me when he called the following evening.

I got home from school the next day and ran into the house at full speed. Coach Custis had told us that all phone calls would come between 4:30 and 5:00 p.m. that night. This was perfect for me because I had soccer practice for my indoor team at 6:00. I stared at the clock in our kitchen nervously. It was 4:30. I tapped my foot against the floor in the kitchen and I must have had six glasses of water. I looked at the clock again, 4:44. I kept convincing myself that he was calling all the guys who got cut first and then all of us who made the team would get our phone calls around five. I waited and waited, and sure enough the phone rang at ten minutes to five. I picked up the receiver on the first ring.

"This is Coach Custis from the Tidal Waves," said the voice on the other end of the phone. "How's it going, Coach?" These were my first words with Coach Custis, besides saying "Uh-huh" to orders he barked at me during tryouts.

"Well, I actually called to tell you that we don't have a spot for you on this year's team. I'm sorry it didn't work out. Don't hang your head though, I want to see you at next year's tryout." Just like that, I was cut from the Tidal Waves.

"Oh, all right, Coach," I tried to fight back tears. "Thanks for calling me and letting me try out for the team."

Coach Custis could tell that I was crying a little. "There's always next year, son, and remember, failure is the mother of all great success. Best of luck with your soccer."

His line about failure being the mother of success might have been true, but I didn't understand what he was talking about. I slammed down the telephone and sunk into the chair, frozen by the news of my sudden dismissal. What had happened? I didn't understand. I began to search for reasons why I had been cut. If only I would have passed more at the beginning. No, if I would have been more aggressive. Wait, was it that shot that I missed on the open net? I thought I showed that I had a good left foot, maybe I didn't show off my right. My mother, who had been giving me space, walked into the kitchen. She gave me a hug and poured me a glass of milk.

"Why did he cut me, Mom?" I was confused.

She spoke softly, without looking away from my eyes. "I don't know, Jimmy. Sometimes things just don't work out. You'll be all right. Let's hope this is the worst thing that ever happens to you." The hushed and saddened sound of her voice told me that seeing me hurt, crushed her as well. "You'll grow from this."

I realized that I was going to have to watch Danny tote around his blue Tidal Waves bag for another year. And all the while, I would have to think about what "could have been." As I sat in the kitchen that evening, I made a very important decision. I would get my Tidal Waves bag next year.

For the first time in my young life, I was finding out how Jimmy Hanks would respond to adversity.

I had soccer practice with my indoor team in a half-hour and I knew that all of my friends would ask about

Tidal Waves tryouts. I would have to tell them I got cut.

I quit crying and stood up. My mother waited for me to say something, but I just stared at the window blankly, thinking. She asked me the question I had been asking myself for the past few minutes, "What do you want to do about indoor practice? You can stay home if you want." She had never offered me that option before. My parents had always taught me that "If you play on a team, then you always go to practice." I paused for a second and wiped my face with my shirt. "I think I want to go, Mom. I'm gonna have to see these guys some time."

I arrived at soccer practice a few minutes early and I saw some of my teammates running toward me. I breathed in deeply. I only hoped that I wouldn't lose my composure and cry in front of all my friends.

"Hey Jimmy," Justin was sprinting to talk to me. "You make the 'Waves?" I collected myself and tried to smile nonchalantly. "No, I got cut," I said. I bit my lip and tried hard not to cry. For a moment, I thought that I'd made the wrong choice by coming to practice. "What? How did *you* get cut? You were awesome."

"I guess that's just the way things go sometimes," I responded.

"Don't worry, I got cut too." He smiled and we walked onto the field together without our Tidal Waves bags.

Chapter 3 : "No Easy Way Out"

I was lying face down in the Florida condominium. Men with handguns looked through my personal possessions like they were wading through piles of garbage. A desperate and terrifying feeling overcame me. I had spent my entire life running, jumping, kicking, shooting, and sliding, and for the first time ever, I couldn't move.

The guy with the green bandanas covering his face, quickly dumped everything out of my Tidal Waves bag and onto the carpeted floor. The first of my things to get tossed was a Sony compact disc player that I had bought two years earlier. My CDs followed, crashing, one by one. The man bent down and picked up a CD. "You've got some nice stuff in here." He picked up a few more, reading through the songs on the front of the discs. "Real nice stuff."

The bandana he wore in front of his mouth was obviously bothering him a little, because I noticed that he continued to re-adjust the position of his disguise. In some strange way this made me very conscious of how human these robbers really were. This thought quickly left my mind as the shining metal of a handgun mesmerized me. Motionless, I watched him drop my CD player and most of my CDs into a big white canvas bag.

He spoke in a tone that matched the hard floors and harsh lighting of our scantily decorated living room. "This stuff is nice, but where's the money?" I thought we had already gone over this. "It's in - " before I could finish my sentence three *hundred and eighty of my crumpled dollars fell onto the floor. The man picked up the cash and threw it into the bag with the rest of my stuff. That was a lot of money for me, half of my Single-A baseball salary for the month. Giving him that money would be a fair trade, as long as he let me out of that condo with my life.*

The two men had been in our place with us now for about fifteen minutes. I was starting to face the very real possibility that this was going to be my last day on earth. I thought about my brothers, Dave and Shawn, and how distraught they would be when they heard that their oldest brother would not be coming back from spring training. And how could my parents face losing a son?

I was surprised to find that I wasn't afraid of dying. I was more afraid of the impact that my death would have on the lives of the people that I cared about. I began thinking of my life back home. Ironically, as the criminals continued shuffling through my soccer bag, a picture of my entire family floated to the floor. The picture was of us at Alfonso's, our favorite Mexican food restaurant. The photo was taken just before my freshman year of high school. I knew as I faced the most traumatic moments of my life, that my family was there with me. I was surprised I remembered that dinner...

Whenever we went out to dinner, Dad would make friends with our waiter or waitress. That night was no different. When the waitress approached the table, Dad had her smiling right away. He told her that we were here to celebrate the beginning of the new school year. She enjoyed his attempt at humor. My brothers and I rolled our eyes and smiled. The small blonde haired waitress handed us five menus and Dad insisted on asking her if there was anything she recommended. She knelt down next to him like they were best friends, and pointed out a few things she liked. Dad does that to people. The first time you meet him, you feel like you've known him forever. I was always proud that he was my father, but his choice to send me to Bayside High School instead of Oceantown Union High School where most of my friends were going, was not making me laugh that night.

The one thing I did have going for me was that I recently became a Tidal Wave on my second attempt. I had made a few close friends on that team who would be starting high school with me at Bayside. Still, I was frightened to be a fourteen year-old freshman at a new school. I didn't want to have an argument at dinner, but I wanted to state my case one last time. "I think it would be much easier if I could just go to school where my friends are. The guys from Bayside don't like the guys from Oceantown, Dad. You know it's not too late to transfer," I knew I would have a hard time winning this argument. "The easy way out" was not part of Dad's vocabulary.

Dad stared across the table at me and spoke softly. "Oceantown's a small place, Jimmy. Everyone you know is from there. You need to get out and meet some new people with different backgrounds, from different places. I expect you to do great things at Bayside." Dad had put his foot down, and that meant I had no choice but to stand up and face his challenge. "I guess I'll make the best of it. I'll go to Bayside." I said grudgingly. "I just hope I can make some friends." I took a sip of my soda and looked up at him, waiting for his endorsement. "I admire your courage," he said. My youngest brother Shawn, the jokester of the family, chimed in, "Yeah Jimmy, real courageous, you're like a superhero." Dave and Shawn started cracking up. I would get my revenge later that night. I was the oldest and the biggest brother. I knew a wedgie or two would shut them up.

I was still not completely sold on the idea of going to Bayside. A surfer boy in an athlete's town, I knew I was in for some trouble. But I wasn't your average "surfer boy." Sure, I had the blonde hair and I wore some crazy shirts. And yes, I liked to say words that fit the surfer stereotype, like "dude" and "bro." But beyond all that stuff, I had a good jump shot, and I could always hit a baseball farther than all my friends. I was excited to show the guys at Bayside that I was just like them. Even if they wouldn't accept me as a friend, they would eventually have to accept me as an athlete.

I arrived at Bayside for my first day of high school. I knew that the surfer look was not a real popular one, but I didn't want to cut my hair or change the way I dressed. I was sure that I would receive plenty of "first day hazing," but I would play the part of the "new kid" with confidence. My hair was long, blonde and parted in the middle. I looked like I had just gotten off a wave and I knew it.

I walked through the double doors at the front entrance of the school and I could feel my heart beating through my shirt. I moved quickly but carefully, surveying the large lobby in search of a friendly face. A few guys looked over at me. They were tall, muscular, and wore varsity letters on their jackets. I gave the guy in the middle a friendly nod, and waited for a response. He wore a pair of dark sunglasses, his hair was slicked back, and he had a girl hanging from his right arm. I definitely wanted this guy to like me. He led his crew of followers over to me, forming a semicircle.

"Hey surfer bro, looks like you made the wrong turn. The beach is that way." He pointed to the girl's bathroom and laughed. "We play real sports at this school. So why don't you grab your surfboard and go back to Oceantown or wherever you're from." His buddies all stood around him and laughed. He wasn't done with me. "Nice hair, maybe we should dye our hair blonde and grow it sideways, then we can be as cool as you." They all started cracking up. I turned my head and silently thought that maybe it was time for a haircut.

I tried to pretend that I wasn't too rattled by these comments, although I was. I faked a smile and walked away from the pack of guys. Just before I turned the corner, I glanced back over my shoulder and the name "Garrett" popped out at me. It was written across the letterman jacket of the guy who had started all the harassment. He had a baseball bat stenciled on the back, so I was sure we'd meet again.

The first five minutes of high school turned out to be exactly what I'd dreaded. Nobody had seen beyond my surfer hair or my Oceantown background. I recalled movies that I had seen where the freshman gets hung from his underwear on a flagpole. I searched the place for flagpoles, and nervously tucked my shirt into my shorts.

I suffered through a rough first couple days of school. The only things I could do to help myself were to get good grades and show up to all my practices on time. Sure, I heard the taunts about being a "surfer boy," but I slowly erased that stereotype when I showcased my athletic ability. Oddly enough, I received more attention on the basketball court than on the soccer field. I always thought soccer would be my sport. Somewhere along the way, I guess things changed.

Despite being cut from the Tidal Waves when I was thirteen years old, I worked as hard as I could to make that team the next year. My perseverance earned me a spot on the 'Waves, and the soccer bag I was rewarded with reminds me of how I fought to turn my failure into a success. Though I made the Tidal Waves, I was hardly a part of that team. Game after game, I learned how to warm benches with the best of them. I had to turn my attention toward a new sport.

I thought basketball was the answer. That year, I played on the junior varsity team as a freshman. Every day, before anyone else showed up at the gym, I would be on the court shooting three pointers. I ran around like a maniac, retrieving the worn out Spalding, and heaving shot after shot at the rim. I loved playing basketball but as a slight one hundred and sixty pound freshman, I had a real tough time banging down low with the "big boys." Although I had a nice jump-shot and was a good ball handler, I didn't have the body to be the player I wanted to be. But basketball did earn me the respect of the athletes at school. All but one of them. I would have to face him on the baseball field.

My success on the freshman baseball team caught the attention of Coach Edmonds, the varsity coach. Between my freshman and sophomore year I was invited to play summer baseball on his team. I hoped that an impressive performance during those months would give me a chance to make the varsity squad as a sophomore.

I was constantly harassed during the practices leading up to our first game, and Tony Garrett was always the first one to fire a cheap shot. At game time, I was formally introduced to my role as the young guy on a team filled with upper-classmen. I had to carry all of the equipment from the bus to the field, and while my teammates warmed up, I was in the dugout filling up cups of water.

I remember the nerves I felt during my first game of summer ball against the Valley Vikings. I had no idea if I would be able to compete at the varsity level, and the thought of embarrassing myself in front of the older guys made my stomach churn. Not to mention the fact that my uniform was a size too big and my sliding pants, made to fit snugly, wore like pajamas. Each time I bent down to scratch an itch, my arms would tangle slightly in my shirt.

I tucked my jersey in and watched the opposing pitcher warm up on the other side of the field. I stared at him as he threw what looked like the fastest pitches I had ever seen outside of a Major League stadium. I continued to look for about three more pitches until I heard, "Hey Hanks, you here to play ball, or take a pitch count?" I thought I recognized that voice. When I turned around, I saw Tony Garrett, the same guy who had been on my case since my very first minute at Bayside. I looked away and jogged to the dugout to retrieve my glove.

When I returned to the field, I paired up with Corey Dunn, one of my friends on the team. We warmed up by tossing the ball around in the outfield. I was trying to show him how to throw a knuckle ball, when suddenly I was interrupted as a ball flew past my face. "Oh, my fault," I heard Tony Garrett say sarcastically. He was smiling from ear to ear, amused by the fright that I had expressed after the ball almost took my ear off. I threw the ball back to him as hard as I could. He caught it and glared at me, "Hey Hanks, do you think that if we just beat you up a few times you could become a part of this team? I mean, right now, you're more like our surfer mascot than our left fielder." This guy never stopped harassing me and I had no idea why. Garrett was the team captain so I would have to put up with his words until I earned his respect inside the lines.

Much to my surprise, Coach Edmonds told me that I would get a chance to pitch a few innings of relief that day. I thought I was an awful pitcher, but I guess I got in there because I could throw hard.

I received an early call to the mound when our starting pitcher was lit up for six runs in the first inning. I figured it would take a dominating pitching performance to quiet Tony Garrett once and for all. As I warmed up, I felt confident. I was throwing hard and hitting all my spots. No one touched base during my first inning of relief. I was actually feeling pretty good until Frank Silvano, a short stocky player on Valley, stepped into the batter's box to open the third. He rocked my first offering up the middle. His single left him standing at first base with nobody out. After I threw a wild pitch to the next batter, Silvano was in scoring position at second base.

The next batter singled, and Silvano tried to score from second. A perfect toss from right field arrived in Kyle Wicks' glove after just one bounce. Kyle caught the ball and waited to apply the tag at home plate. Silvano was going to be out by at least five feet. Instead of slowing up, which would have been appropriate baseball etiquette, Silvano sped up and slid into home plate with his cleats high. Wicks tagged him out easily, but paid the price. The two players tumbled over one another as Silvano's spikes ripped through Kyle's pants, tearing a large patch of unprotected skin stretching six inches across his inner thigh. A stream of blood came pouring down his leg, and he had to be carried off the field. It was the most gruesome scene I had ever witnessed on a baseball field. To our dismay, Silvano only received a warning from the umpire, and remained in the game. We were left to find redemption for our fallen comrade.

After the inning had ended, Tony Garrett pulled me aside in the dugout with a hard look on his face. His word on the diamond was much like Coach's and was not to be contested. I listened closely. He was the kind of guy that stood behind his teammates and I knew he wouldn't let Silvano get away with such a malicious slide without some sort of payback.

Tony grabbed me by the collar of my shirt and pulled me to about three inches from his face. I could taste his lunch. His eyes looked like they were ready to burst out of his head. "Listen to me, kid. When Silvano comes up again, I want you to hit him with a fastball as hard as you can. Nobody gets away with that garbage!" I listened to what Tony was saying, and I thought about his words for a few seconds. I didn't want to throw at anyone. Garrett saw my discomfort and knew that I wasn't completely on board with his plan. "And Hanks, you can be sure that if you don't peg him, you're going to have to deal with me. If you want to be a part of this team, then it's time you prove it." He slammed a baseball down hard into the center of my mitt and walked towards the water cooler, where he filled up two cups and drank them both.

I was hoping that Coach would pull me out of the game before Silvano came to the plate. I didn't want to deal with the situation. But as I moved through the order, I made the realization that Coach had no intention of pulling me off the mound. Silvano was in the on-deck circle with just one out in the sixth. I knew I was going to have to pitch to him. I was faced with a difficult decision. If I didn't throw at Silvano, I would never have had a chance to gain the respect of Tony Garrett. I also knew that Garrett would probably fight me if I didn't hit Silvano. Part of me felt like Silvano deserved a fastball in his side, but the other part of me didn't want to be the guy to deliver the pitch. There was no easy way out.

Silvano came to home plate and I made a huge mistake. I turned and looked right at Tony. He was pacing back and forth, kicking up dirt, and punching his mitt as hard as he could. He stared at me. He looked like a crazed bull and I could almost see the steam coming out of his nostrils. I knew what I had to do, peg Silvano.

My control was real good that day and I figured I would be able to harmlessly plunk him in the leg with a fastball. The intentional knockdown would serve as retaliation for our injured teammate, and I hoped the payback would get Tony off my case once and for all. I took the sign from our new catcher, and nodded in approval. I wound up and tossed the ball toward home plate.

The two-seamer was headed right for Silvano's midsection. He attempted to dodge the pitch but it was too late. The ball smacked him in the hip. A few of the players on the Vikings stirred in the dugout, but no one budged. They knew that this was the etiquette of the game. I didn't throw near his head, and I protected my teammates with class. Silvano fired his bat to the dirt and stared at me while he walked to first. I knew he was in some pain and I felt bad, but not as bad as I felt for Kyle, who was bleeding in the emergency room.

The umpire threw me back another baseball, and I turned and looked at Tony. He nodded his head and touched the bill of his cap, a gesture of thank you in the game of baseball. I think he even smiled.

I went on to retire the side easily. Tony ran past me and patted me on the back, "Nice job, Hanks." His days of hazing me had come to an end.

Chapter 4 : "The Umbrella Man"

I stared at the closed blinds for a few long moments, losing focus on what was actually happening. My mind kept wandering as the bandana-covered man shuffled through the rest of my belongings. He dumped everything I had out of my soccer bag and onto the floor. The three hundred and eighty dollars that he had thrown into his white bag was going to be my rent money for the month. I wondered if I would ever pay that bill again. I wondered if the last thing I would see during my life, would be the white vertical blinds blowing lightly in the breeze of an over air-conditioned Florida condominium.

The robber who'd been quiet for the past few minutes while he manned the door, suddenly spoke, "All right, I want everyone's face touching that carpet. I'm sick of having you people stare at me." He was a little more abrupt with us than his counterpart.

We did what he said and plastered our faces to the floor. The bright lights of matching couch-side lamps were gone, and just like that, there was darkness. Not being able to see what was happening made my hearing extremely sensitive. I could hear one of the men moving around the room impatiently. I heard a suitcase being unzipped on the other side of the bed. Clothes were being thrown into piles on the floor. I could hear the men shuffling through the shirts and pants, complaining that we all had terrible taste. And then I was happy for a moment. I realized that none of my stuff would fit these guys. I was six feet tall and each of them stood only about five foot-

five. A small victory for the good guys.

"You," the man's voice was still close. None of us were sure who he was speaking to. I peeked my head up for an instant, making sure it wasn't me. "You," he repeated himself a little louder. An answer followed immediately, "Me?" That was the voice of Nick Erickson.

One word and I remembered a thousand conversations we'd had. Nick, a long time friend from high school, was also trying to survive on the arduous road to the Majors. He was lying down directly behind me, my foot brushed against his shoulder. The man pushed Nick on the back and I could feel him flinch. "Empty your pockets."

Nick turned slowly and reached into the pocket of his jeans. "Here, take it." His hushed tone sounded like home to me. And in an otherwise silent room, hearing him speak made me feel a quiet calm. With Nick just a few feet away, I couldn't help but recall a talk we'd had when I was fifteen years old. That talk changed my life. Without his encouragement, I may not have ever played professional baseball. Nick was the first person who ever called me a ballplayer...

"Jimmy, I know you love basketball. But I don't understand why you don't just concentrate on playing baseball, you could really be awesome." Nick told me this as we sat on my couch playing a hockey video game. I gave him a strange look, scored a goal, and prepared myself for an intense conversation. He pretended not to notice that I'd scored. "All I'm saying is that basketball's kind of a waste of time. It's not like you're going to play in the NBA." He spoke in an animated fashion while Mario

Lemieux skated down the ice and nailed a slap shot toward the upper right corner of my goal. The goalie didn't make the play and I blamed my bum controller. Nick wasn't buying my excuse, and insisted on showing me the replay. We never stopped competing.

I knew I wasn't going to be a professional basketball player, but that wasn't why I started playing in the first place. I tried to get this point across to Nick, "I'm not trying to get to the NBA or the Major Leagues. I just love playing both sports." This made a lot of sense, and Nick was rendered silent for a moment.

"I saw you play basketball this season, and you were good. But think about baseball, you made the varsity squad during summer ball, and that was only after your freshman year. If we practice hard, we could take this all the way. Imagine that? Jimmy Hanks and Nick Erickson, Major League Baseball players?" His face lit up as he confessed his dream to me. I stared at the screen blankly, and then looked over at Nick. "Yeah right."

Listening to Nick was actually starting to change the way I approached my future in baseball. Maybe I did have a chance. He continued on, "If you start dedicating yourself to baseball now, then you can play in college. You play well there, who knows! I mean you've got to think about your future." I shut off the video game, brought out a bag of chips, and moved into the kitchen. Nick had gotten me thinking. I responded to his comments with the greatest weapon I had against him, logic. "You know we probably have like a one in a million chance at playing sports for a living. Seriously Nick, I like the odds of getting a college education much better." I wasn't finished. "I'm gonna go to San Diego University. I mean, that's my plan at least. I'll study hard there, and then I'm going to be a banker like my Dad."

As much as I loved playing sports, I knew I had a better chance of becoming an astronaut than I did of becoming a professional baseball player. I decided that the only logical thing to do was dream quietly. And as the days and nights went by, my dreams were soon all about baseball. Even in my sleep I was becoming a ballplayer. Although outwardly I would laugh at Nick for dreaming, mentally, I was plotting my own road to the Majors. Every day, Nick's words echoed in my head, "You are too good at baseball to be playing another sport...If you play well in college, who knows? Imagine that, Jimmy Hanks, a Major League Baseball player?" I did imagine, and as my junior year in high school rolled around, I started wondering if basketball was really worth my time.

Nick was always talking about our junior year. This was the big one. "If you're gonna have a good baseball season, do it when you're a junior."

After a strong sophomore campaign in which I batted .328, I was sure someone would notice me during the upcoming year. But the pressure I put on myself to get a hit every time I came to the plate was too much, and my confidence soured with each out that I made. My average hovered around .260 and I couldn't figure out what was wrong. Despite my ice-cold bat, our team still managed to make the playoffs. Our first round game was against Kingston High School.

The California sky was gray that day, and for one of the first times in my baseball life, I had to wear a long sleeve shirt underneath my uniform. Fog had rolled into the outfield, and the layers of white were so thick that I could barely see the pitcher's mound. I noticed that only a few damp spectators remained in the stands. A light rain had scared the rest away. I walked into the dugout and sat on the bench next to Nick, who was staring into the bleachers intently. I approached him. "Hey, you believe that fog?"

As usual, Nick was in his own world. "What?"

I noticed him staring into the stands. "Are you looking for someone?"

"Nope. Just hoping someone's looking for me." Nick pointed to a few remaining spectators in the nearly vacant stands. "Let's see, from right to left, we've got the assistant coach from the University of Long Beach, and the other two guys are Major League scouts." Nick liked to know which scouts were at our games. A baseball scout is a person sent to recruit a player for college or professional baseball. Personally, having them there made me kind of nervous.

I noticed a few faces that Nick hadn't mentioned. "Who are those two guys in the third row, right behind my mom?"

Nick couldn't see them from his vantage point. He leaned his head forward. "Which guys?" I pointed to the two men I was talking about. They sat a few feet apart from one another, silently scribbling onto their notepads. I wasn't sure if they knew each other. "The one on the left looks like he might be wearing a San Diego University jacket, and who's that other guy with the huge umbrella?" I was seeing SDU paraphernalia everywhere lately. "Every guy wearing blue isn't a SDU coach, Jimmy." I guess I was obsessed with the Sharks. Nick stood up to get a closer look, "I actually don't know who those guys are."

We took some quick infield practice before the game

started. In between throws from third base, I did a quick scan of the bleachers, looking to see if the man with the blue jacket was, in fact, a SDU recruiter. I waved to my mom, who was clapping her hands in front of the man in question. Then I made a nice back-handed stop on a short-hop off the bat of Coach Custis. After I fired the ball across the diamond, I saw that royal blue baseball jacket again. I couldn't make out whether or not there was a SDU logo on it. I stared as hard as I could, and my mom kept waving, thinking I was looking at her. I still couldn't decide if he was an SDU scout, or if my imagination was in overdrive. A hard grounder shot past my glove into left field. I turned my head to follow the one that had gotten away when Coach Custis yelled out, "Heads up over there Jimmy, let's go." I tried to refocus on infield practice, but I couldn't stop staring into the stands. Every time I would catch a glimpse of the man's hat, or the breast pocket of his jacket, my mother would change positions and block my view. On top of that, the man with the oversized blue and gray umbrella kept twirling his ridiculous rain gear in circles above his head, further blocking my view.

Coach hit me another grounder. This one I fielded cleanly, but the muddy ball slipped through my fingers, causing my throw to sail high above the head of our first baseman. I was sure the man in the blue jacket was hardly impressed. After two straight errors, I began hoping he wasn't a SDU scout after all.

When I peered back into the stands, I noticed my mother was gone. The rain had picked up a little and I guess she had moved to her car for shelter. I finally had a clear shot at the man in blue. I was right all along. The SDU logo on the pocket of his jacket

44

jumped out at me like my brothers would from behind a door. The man wearing the jacket was Larry Diaz, the assistant baseball coach at San Diego University. I had been attending SDU games since I was a little kid so I immediately recognized the small man with a dark complexion to be Coach Diaz. I quickly looked away from him, fielded a tough grounder to my left and made a strong throw to first. After the play, I noticed Mr. Diaz speaking with the "umbrella man." I wondered if the owner of the umbrella was affiliated with SDU as well.

I ignored this question. It was time to focus on baseball, and as Coach would say, "Those guys in the stands can't help you, you've got to do this job yourself." I knew the moment had arrived, "Game time."

Kingston opened the scoring with six runs in the first four innings. The cold air hadn't chilled their hot bats, but it had certainly cooled ours. By the time we came to the plate in the bottom of the fourth, we trailed 6-0. The vibe in our dugout was one of despair. We all knew that we were twelve outs away from another long off-season. It was like watching the end of a movie, and seeing the curtains rapidly close before our eyes. With our season on the line, Tony Garrett came to the plate. He swung at an 0-1 fastball and drilled the two-seamer just over the shortstop's head. He'd opened the curtains back up. The movie wasn't over just yet.

Nick followed Tony's lead, lacing a double past the diving first baseman and into the right field corner. Our bats had come alive. Suddenly, our entire team was standing up and making noise. They began shaking at the metal links that guarded the dugout. Everyone was so riled up I feared the fence would come down.

There were runners on second and third when I walked to the plate. I glanced over my shoulder and noticed that Larry Diaz and his umbrella-toting friend were now standing. I dug into the batter's box, staring at my grip. The first pitch nearly clipped my head, and I stood up without dusting myself off, an intimidating trick I learned from the movie, *Major League*. The next pitch was low and outside, and the count stood at 2-0 in my favor. At 2-0, I changed my mentality and looked for a pitch that I could drive someplace. The next offering was a belt high fastball, right down the center of the plate. It was the kind of pitch that screamed "hit me." I listened to the scream and cranked one to left. The ball easily cleared the ten-foot fence. My homerun chopped Kingston's lead in half. Kingston 6, Bayside 3.

The momentum had swung in our favor. When I came to bat in the bottom of the sixth, we trailed by only one. The tying run stood on third base with one out. All I needed was a deep fly ball, and the game would be tied up. This was "do-or-die" time. Our playoff lives were resting on my not-so broad shoulders.

The first pitch was a curve ball over the outside corner, strike one. I had been looking for a fastball and the off speed pitch really fooled me. I had to tip my hat to the pitcher. The next pitch was a low fastball that I golfed to left field. I knew as soon as I made contact that I'd hit one deep enough to tie the game. I sprinted toward first base as the left fielder gauged the distance of my fly ball. He began fading toward the wall, waiting for my deep fly to land in his glove. He slowly began running out of real estate, reaching the limits of the field. When I saw his back slam against the fence, I knew the ball had a chance to go out. The lanky outfielder leaped, but came up empty handed. I'd hit another homerun. Bayside 7, Kingston 6.

After I rounded the bases I was greeted at home plate by my teammates, who began slapping the top of my helmet. The scene was pure pandemonium and I was at the center of the celebration! Even Tony Garrett, my old enemy, hugged me. Nick slapped my helmet hard enough to make my ears ring. "Hey! I told you, you were a ballplayer, didn't I?" He was right, I was a ballplayer. I only hoped that Larry Diaz thought the same thing.

Somehow, we had extended our season. We came from the depths to eliminate a six run deficit and win the game. As we shook hands and slapped five on the infield grass, Kingston packed up their stuff for summer.

I walked over to the dugout to get my gear and go home. I was taking off my cleats when I noticed Larry Diaz walking down the steps of our dugout. This was not what I expected. I wondered if he was really coming in to talk to me. My heart raced. I jumped up, barefoot, excited to greet him. As he walked down the steps, I imagined myself in an SDU uniform once again. I had been waiting years for this moment. He reached out to shake my hand, "Heck of a game, Jimmy."

I was nervous, "Thank you sir, I— "

"Oh, there's Silver, right there." He pointed to the end of the bench where Jake Silver, our star pitcher, was picking the mud out of his cleats. Mr. Diaz patted me on the shoulder and moved past me. He had come to see Silver, not me. I quickly fired everything into my baseball bag, and hurried barefoot out of the dugout. I had been duped. Two home runs, one a game winner, and all I got was a pat on the back.

Jake Silver sat with Larry Diaz, and the two joked around like they were war buddies. I was the odd man out.

I walked to the parking lot alone. I tried not to be too upset, heck, I just played the game of my life. This made being shunned even more difficult to swallow. On top of all that, the floodgates opened up. The rain started coming down in buckets, soaking my cap, my clothes, and my spirit. I stared at my muddy feet and watched water pour off the brim of my cap. I wanted to go home.

A voice came from nowhere, "Hey, you always walk barefoot in the rain?" I looked up and noticed the "umbrella-man" leaning against the side door of my truck. He was still twirling his umbrella like Mary Poppins. Who was this guy? Despite his friendly smile, I still had a bad taste in my mouth from Larry Diaz.

"Can I help you with something?" I snapped at the man.

"Maybe I can help you. Get under this umbrella." He spoke in a comforting tone.

I noticed a Major League emblem on the man's umbrella. I immediately moved underneath with him. The once mysterious "umbrella man" was a tall, well built African American man in his early thirties. He extended his large hand out to me with a smile. He looked like an athlete, albeit, one that had passed his prime a few years ago. We shook hands as he spoke. "Well Jimmy, Coach Edmonds sure has a lot of good things to say about you. I'm Roger Davie, a scout for Seattle. It's nice to meet you." I was shocked that the stranger knew who I was.

This was the first Major League scout that I had ever met in person, and I wasn't sure exactly what I was supposed to say. My voice was shaky and my words were high-pitched. "Nice to meet you, sir." We stood about six inches apart from one another as the rain crashed down all around us.

Mr. Davie grabbed control of the conversation, "I scout the West Coast for Seattle. I actually came here today to take a look at Nick Erickson. He's a fine ballplayer."

I was happy for Nick, but was I about to get overlooked again? "He sure is. He's a great guy too," I said. Mr. Davie playfully kicked water from a large puddle that had formed around my truck. "To tell you the truth Jimmy, I was equally impressed with you. I think you swing a very mature bat. I don't see that kind of patience in a high school hitter too often." This was unbelievable. I must have said "thank you" five times.

He continued, "Keep this stuff up. Who knows, you could be a draft pick for Seattle this June." A draft pick? For a Major League Baseball team? I knew I had to say something. "Mr. Davie, I don't know what to say." That was all I could come up with.

Roger reached into his back pocket and pulled out an index card with a Seattle logo in the corner. He laughed a little, sensing how excited I was. "Just keep up with your schoolwork and keep playing baseball as hard as you can. And here," he handed me the card, "try to keep this dry. We'll be in touch."

Chapter 5: "Back on Track"

Nick and I lay still as the man with the green bandanas pestered him. "This is really all you got?" I heard Nick shuffling through his pockets. "Yeah, I – ".

"And you're sure that's it?" The man repeated himself. "You need to get a night job or something." He crouched down closer to us on the floor and moved to a few inches away from Nick's face. "I'm joking. That's funny, man. You can laugh at that, can't you?" I thought it took a lot of gall for a criminal to joke with us about having a job.

"That's everything I have," Nick said, without any emotion in his voice. He was not amused by the man's poor attempt at humor.

The robber continued around the room and I began to get sick of trying to figure out where he was and what he was doing. I stopped looking for him out of the corners of my eyes. I began to realize that these men could kill us as easily as they were robbing us. Had I really come this far in my life to have everything end now?

I think at that exact moment, when I posed this question to myself, I began to space out. I wasn't listening to the men's voices anymore, and for a few minutes, I wasn't really there. I could hear the air-conditioner, the sound of cars parking below came through clearly, and the television blared in the background. I could hear everyone breathing all around me, living out their private nightmares as I lived out mine. The sounds started to form patterns, and soon, I was daydreaming.

Pictures and thoughts that hadn't entered my brain in years began to parade through my mind as clearly as if they'd happened only a moment earlier.

I started remembering my life in awesome moments. I remembered kindergarten, rolling toy trucks through the sandbox with my best friend, Doug Bird. I could remember him smiling the same way he did years later on the baseball field. I remembered Dad and I sitting across from one another, drinking hot chocolate at the top of the ski slope. And then I was nine years old, standing up for the first time on my surfboard, waves crashing in front of me and behind. I felt like I was actually there. My board was blue and covered with stickers that I probably would laugh at today. That thing carried me like I was walking on water. I jumped off my surfboard, and for some reason I was at Stacey Wagman's birthday party in the seventh grade. I'd spiked my hair to impress her, and I think the extra gel really worked, because she sat down next to me on a light brown couch. I always had a crush on Stacey.

I remembered driving my black pickup truck, my first, and favorite car. I had passed the driving test for my license, and when I came home, my friends were waiting for me with their thumbs out, like they were hitching a ride. We fit about six of us into my tiny pickup, drove over to Big-Bite Burgers and stuffed ourselves until we were all sick. The scene was so real, I could almost taste the burgers, and hear the laughter from my friends.

My memory put me back on my surfboard. I remembered cheering for Dave at his soccer game, hanging out with

52

Shawn on our deck, driving with my friends to parties, laughing with Mom, playing baseball, and then I was walking out to the mailbox in an SDU t-shirt...

I was lying across our living room couch, flipping channels, and eating chips, wondering why my junior season had been such a disappointment. Despite my heroics against Kingston, the rest of that year was a complete nightmare. Our team had a nice run in the playoffs, but we were simply outmatched by Liberty in the third round.

On this particular Saturday, two days after our season ended, I decided I would hang out at home and watch some basketball on television. The NBA finals were in full swing and Michael Jordan's Bulls looked poised to add another ring to their collection. I could watch MJ play all day long.

I was feeling sort of down because I hadn't been selected to play in the summer Connie Mack League or the Area Code games. The top high school players in Southern California compete in these two leagues, and at each game, the stands are filled with college coaches and professional scouts. I realized that my junior statistics, a mediocre .256 average and a measly four home runs, hadn't turned any coaches' heads. I just hoped that Coach Edmonds' campaigning for me, and memories of my strong sophomore season, would get me an invitation to one of the two leagues. But when the calls were made, my phone never rang. I was hurt - - almost devastated. I was forced to play another summer of American Legion ball, where the scouts were few and far between.

I wondered if I had any future in baseball at all. I ate a

few more handfuls of potato chips and watched Michael Jordan wag his tongue and soar through the air for two more points. He'd been cut from *his* high school team, and he was the best basketball player ever. I still had a chance.

I sat up sharply, shut off the television, and rose to my feet. I called out to anyone who would listen. "Has anyone gotten the mail, yet?" I screamed this a few times across the house, but no one answered. I was grumpy, and annoyed that nobody could hear me, "I'll get it."

I remember that walk to the mailbox. I opened the front door to our house, and stretched as if I'd been asleep for days. I looked up at the sky, another beautiful day in Oceantown. I had a blue SDU shirt on and my hat was turned backwards.

I opened our mailbox carelessly, pulling out a big pile of envelopes. I was really interested in the mail lately because Nick told me how he was getting all these letters from different colleges about playing baseball. But each time I had gone to my mailbox, I returned empty handed. Some school in America must have at least *heard* of Jimmy Hanks.

After I saw that the first few items weren't for me, I lost my original excitement. I routinely flipped through the envelopes and magazines. A bill for mom, Surfer Magazine for Dave and me, a few bills for Dad, a letter for the Hanks family, another couple of bills, a letter for me from SDU, another bill for Dad. Wait, a letter for me from SDU. A letter, for me? From SDU? There was a big SDU emblem in the upper left-hand corner of the envelope, and below it were the words, "San Diego University Athletic Department."

I ran back into the house, tripping over my sweatpants, and losing my baseball hat somewhere between the front door and the kitchen table. I frantically dropped all the other mail onto the counter and stood staring at my SDU letter. After a few seconds of heavy breathing, I opened up the envelope carefully. There was a short note inside. I read it aloud.

"Dear Jimmy:

The San Diego University baseball coaches have taken notice of your high school accomplishments. Your baseball skills could some day earn you a spot on the SDU baseball team. Our program looks forward to following your progress in the upcoming summer and into next season. Enclosed is an information card that will help us keep in contact with you. Please fill out this card and send it back to us as soon as possible. We wish you the best of luck in the future.

Sincerely,

Larry Diaz
Assistant Coach
SDU Baseball

SDU had taken notice of me. After that day in the dugout against Kingston, I thought Larry Diaz wanted nothing to do with me. Now I had received a letter from the most storied college baseball program in the country. I didn't know if these letters went out to high school ballplayers every day, but to be perfectly honest, I didn't care. This was the first time a college had noticed me, and the letter was from the only school I ever wanted to attend.

My two uncles went to SDU, my grandfather went to school there, and in the sixth grade, I decided that SDU was where I would go to college. In San Diego, you're either a SDU family or a Pacific College family, and our family was always die-hard SDU. I didn't care how ordinary that letter was. I was going to play baseball at San Diego University.

I filled out the information card in about three minutes and drove down to the post office to get that thing in the mail as fast as I could. Suddenly, my baseball career was back on track.

I realized that I needed to put up staggering numbers during my senior year to keep SDU interested. I was determined to show everyone, including myself, that I was a much better ballplayer than my junior season indicated.

A couple of days before my senior baseball season started, I headed down to the local basketball court to clear my brain. The previous season, I had gotten so caught up in the hype of the recruiting process that my play on the field suffered dramatically. I thought a few jump shots would loosen me up. I missed the first three that I took and decided I needed to move in a few steps to find my range. I dribbled toward the hoop and fired a one handed jumper that clanked off the front of the rim. My momentum pushed me forward and the ball shot over my head. When I turned around to get the rebound, I saw Roger Davie, the "umbrella man."

"Mr. Davie? What are you doing here?" He collected my rebound and was cradling the ball against his hip. I shook his hand, confused as to what brought him onto my neighborhood court.

"I just went by your house and your mom told me I could find you here. I always carry some hoops clothes in my trunk." I noticed he had turned in his umbrella for a pair of mesh basketball shorts, high tops, and a blue knee brace. Mr. Davie bounced my ball in between his legs. "You ready?"

"Ready for what, Mr. Davie?" I was puzzled.

"Call me Roger."

"O.k. Roger. So what should I be ready for?"

"Getting your butt kicked." Roger spun the basketball on his finger and started laughing. "I hear you're a heck of a basketball player. But I can play a little ball myself."

"Are you serious? You want to play me?" Now I was laughing.

He fired the ball at my chest. "Check it up." He *was* serious. A professional baseball scout wanted to play me in basketball? I couldn't believe this.

"To eleven, counting by ones, win by two," I was speaking basketball lingo.

"All right," I checked the ball in as Roger set his feet in a defensive stance. I began dribbling toward him. I head faked to my left, dribbled once in that direction, and then quickly crossed the ball back to my right hand. Roger lunged for the steal and I blew right by him for an easy lay-up.

"What happened there?" I jokingly asked Roger.

"Shut up. That won't happen again." He was a little embarrassed, but that didn't keep him from smiling.

"One-zero, me." Again, I dribbled directly toward him, but this time, even faster. He retreated onto his back foot. That gave me all the separation I needed. Roger tried to regain his balance and put a hand in my face. He was a step slow and I calmly drained a fourteen-foot jump shot. Two-nothing.

"What's up now, Roger?" I was starting to have some fun. I didn't think some friendly trash talk would hurt.

"Hey, that's enough out of you," Roger said, trying to be serious while his smile crept through. "You should remember that I'm a scout for Seattle. A team that *was* thinking of picking you in the draft until a few seconds ago." Roger started laughing.

The rest of the game continued in much of the same fashion. The final score was 11-1. Roger was a good sport despite the blowout. "You whipped me pretty good, kid," he said as we began walking back to my house.

We trekked up a steep hill as cars passed by us. "Why did you want to play me in basketball anyway?" I asked him.

"I wanted to see what kind of athlete you are," he replied.

"And?" I asked.

"You're an athlete," Roger said as he wiped the sweat from his forehead.

When the two of us got back to my house, Mom made us some lemonade. We sat on the couch and talked like we were old pals. We spoke about baseball and we wondered who would win it all this year. We talked about school, girls, and college. I mentioned to him that I wanted to go to SDU and he gave his approval.

That afternoon, Roger convinced me that my Major League dream could come true. "It will be the hardest thing you ever have to do in your life, but I see something in you," he told me. "Now you just gotta want it more than anybody else." Roger believed in me when very few did, and I would never forget that. On that day, I dedicated myself to becoming a Major League baseball player.

Chapter 6: "Blaine Field"

Talk about a great day gone bad. A few hours earlier we had been promoted to Double-A, now we'd be lucky if we survived the night. I was angry that these men stole this day from us. We should've been celebrating our promotion to Amarillo together, not sharing scared looks.

If these men had any sort of humanity behind their dark masks and weapons, they would simply take our money and run. They had robbed us, and we hadn't given them any problems. So why weren't they leaving?

As these thoughts raced through my mind I heard a car door slam shut just outside of our front door. I hoped someone had looked into our window, noticed the five of us on the floor, and called the police. I prayed that state troopers were waiting outside, ready to bust the criminals. A moment later there was a light knocking on the door.

The man who had been guarding the exit looked out of the peep hole. "It's a pizza delivery guy, what do we do?" He nervously asked his partner.

After thirty minutes, the pizza-man had finally arrived. In the heat of this terrifying experience, I completely forgot that dinner was on its way.

Suddenly, the criminal running the robbery grabbed me by the shirt collar and yanked me up to my feet. "You, answer the door. And here, take this," he threw me a twenty-dollar bill, "don't you even think about making this guy think something's wrong. You play it cool or it's gonna get real ugly in here."

*I knew what my assignment was. I was to go to the
door, trade the twenty dollars for the pizzas, and make believe
that there was nothing unusual about this exchange. If I made
a false move, somebody was going to pay for it. I walked toward the door and opened it.*

*"Fifteen dollars and forty four cents," the delivery boy
was sporting his Mama Mia's hat backwards and his eyes
hardly strayed from the two boxes he handed me. I wanted him
to look into my eyes and see the fear, the terror. I hoped he
would notice my shaky hand, or my pale expression, or the
fact that I was breathing like I had just run the Boston Marathon. But he didn't. To him, this was just another delivery. I
needed to do something. This could be our only chance at an
escape, I thought. As I handed him the twenty dollar bill and
insisted he keep the change, I mouthed the word "help" as
clearly as I could.*

*"What?" the pizza guy asked with a strange look on
his face. I tried to mouth the word again, but just as I was
about to, I felt a heavy gun poking into my ribs. One of the
criminals was hiding behind the door, monitoring my every
move. I jolted upright, realizing that I could have just made a
costly mistake. The delivery boy looked concerned, "Hey, are
you alright buddy?"*

*Just as he finished those words, the criminal closed the
door, locked it, and threw me to the floor. "You know how
close you just came to getting yourself shot? Now stay down
on the floor!" The man with the black ski mask brought the*

pizza over to our kitchen table and began eating it in front of us. Not only were they holding us up, but they were humiliating us by eating our pizza in front of our faces. The man with the green bandanas walked over to us licking his fingers, and pointing his pistol at us.

"All right, everybody put your hands behind your back," he spoke sternly.

I followed his orders cautiously. A moment later, I heard the unraveling of duct tape. This sound was followed by a few deep sighs from some of the guys, and a short groan from Chad. To this day, the sound of duct tape unraveling makes me cringe.

The larger of the two men grabbed my hands and yanked them together, putting tape over and around my wrists as tight as he possibly could. Again and again, he circled my wrists with tape, until I couldn't feel my fingers. My hands began to throb with pain.

A moment later he bent over me and whispered into my ear forcefully, "Talk about being in the wrong place at the wrong time, huh?" The wrong place at the wrong time. He was absolutely right. These words were strange to me. Until today, I'd always had pretty good timing. I remembered playing baseball at Blaine Field when I was eighteen years old. Talk about the right place at the right time...

Coach Edmonds insisted that the key to getting recruited was simple: be at the right place at the right time, and go three for four with a homer. He always laughed when he told me this, but he was right. When the scouts are watching, you have to play well. During my senior season, I finally put everything together. I played the best baseball of my young life, yet no college coaches called. My .444 batting average was the highest on our team and the third highest in the county. Still, SDU hadn't contacted me since that letter arrived a year ago. I began to wonder if they had forgotten about me.

In the middle of my senior season, Coach Edmonds called SDU's head baseball coach, Mark Jessup, to tell him that I was a guy he was willing to endorse. I continued crushing the ball throughout the season, but Coach Jessup never called back. In fact, no one called, not even one college coach.

Early that spring, I received news that my 3.5 grade point average had earned me an academic acceptance letter to SDU. It's an excellent college academically, and I would have a chance to study finance at one of the most prestigious business schools in the country. I had my ticket to be a Shark, but not as a baseball player. At the end of my senior year, when everyone talked about which school they would be attending, I sat quietly and wondered if playing on the SDU baseball team was even a possibility. Doug Bird was going to study medicine at Duane University, and Nick Erickson had earned a baseball scholarship to the University of New York, a very competitive Division I program. My two best friends' dreams had both come true, while mine had been put on hold.

That summer I decided I would focus all my attention on fine tuning my baseball skills. I'd have to get bigger and stronger to compete at the next level and that was exactly what I did. For the first time in my life, I began lifting weights and I started bulking up. I put on ten pounds of muscle and my six-foot frame was now carrying a hefty two hundred pounds. I was in the best shape of my life. The weightlifting added a new dimension to my game, power. I started blasting balls out of the park like it was my job. I began using my legs as my main source of power, and my swing was a little different, more compact and powerful.

Coach Morris, my American Legion coach during the summer after my senior season, also made a phone call to SDU on my behalf. Coach Jessup told him that he didn't have any scholarship money left for me, but that I was welcome to try and walk on the team. Translation: The SDU baseball program did not think I was as good as the players they were recruiting. However, Coach Morris did convince Coach Jessup to send Larry Diaz to watch me play another game. I figured this might be my last chance to impress him.

Coach Morris told me that Larry Diaz would be in the stands for our playoff game at North Beach's Blaine Field. Blaine Field was an absolutely enormous ballpark with Major League dimensions. There were a few theories about the field. Some people said that the coastal marine layer kept balls in the yard, while others claimed that the dimensions of the park were actually bigger than the numbers written on the fences. Coach Morris told us to try and hit line drives, because a fly ball at Blaine Field had no realistic chance of leaving the ballpark.

The game was about to start and I had knots in my stomach. After all, this could be my last baseball game ever. If we were eliminated and no colleges came calling, I would have no choice but to hang up my cleats. I playfully dug my spikes into the dirt near the third base bag. In the stands, people were settling into their seats. I realized that the next time I was at a baseball game, I might be the spectator. My dad was sitting a few rows above the dugout. He looked over at me and gave an enthusiastic fist pump. He knew how much this game meant.

When we came back to the dugout for our first "licks," I noticed Larry Diaz standing behind the backstop. He was using his radar gun to clock San Miguel's pitcher, "Big Boned" Lionel Strone. Larry was there as a favor to Coach Morris, but he wouldn't waste the opportunity to scout Strone, who had earned his nickname because of his enormous two hundred fifty-pound frame. He threw real hard, over ninety miles per hour. I watched him very carefully. I was starting to understand the game better and I noticed something when our lead-off hitter took a 3–2 breaking ball for a called strike three. Whenever Strone threw anything besides a fastball, he would fiddle with the ball in his glove for a much longer period of time. On the other hand, when he was going to throw a fastball, he would simply wind up and deliver. Strone was tipping off every one of his pitches. I told the guys on the bench about his tendency before I left the dugout for the on-deck circle.

There were runners on first and second when I came to bat that inning. I had Strone figured out. On the first pitch, he didn't play with the ball in his glove, he just looked at the sign and got ready to throw. I knew what was coming, a fastball. That didn't matter much though; the pitch came so far inside that I nearly lost an eye. I jumped backwards and fell to the floor.

The second pitch was a real good curve ball. I swung and missed, almost falling down again. I glanced back at Larry Diaz accidentally. I knew I looked bad on that pitch.

The next pitch was a fastball, I could tell because Strone never hesitated. This one looked like a strike and I was ready and waiting. But instead of taking my usual stride forward and attacking the baseball, I did something a little different. When I saw this pitch, I reached back for more. I shifted the entire weight of my body onto my back foot, coiling my bat a little further back behind my head, and summoning all of the power I could into hitting that baseball. The next thing I heard was the "ping" of the aluminum bat.

I remember hearing Rick Ciccione's deep voice from our bench as soon as I made contact, "Oh my God." He sounded like he'd seen a car accident or something.

I ran as hard as I could down the first base line, hoping that the ball would have enough juice to be out of the center fielder's reach. I was thinking double all the way.

The ball climbed higher and higher into the blue sky, and right as I touched first base, I realized that this blast was not coming back. I slowed my pace and stopped racing, as I watched the ball land well over the wall in center field. I had nailed one over the 400-foot sign in center field. I had homered at the Grand Canyon of all baseball parks, Blaine Field.

The crowd wasn't necessarily loud after my hit, I think they were too confused to make any noise. I could hear some voices in the stands, conversations, a horn blew loudly, someone screamed my name, and then I heard some applause. As I rounded third base, most of the crowd was standing, and I remember Coach Morris' eyes were as wide as if he'd seen a ghost. He slapped me on the back as I ran past him.

A moment later the guys were bumping chests with me, and pushing me around like a rag-doll. I had fired everyone up and I knew that unless Larry Diaz made an emergency trip to the bathroom or a nearby hot dog vendor, I had SDU's attention once again. I leaned back and smiled, this was my moment. Larry Diaz had now seen me play two games and I had three home runs in five at-bats.

I walked out to play shortstop in the bottom half of the first inning and routinely took a few ground balls that our first baseman threw my way. I looked behind the backstop and noticed that Larry Diaz was no longer there. Had he missed my mammoth homer? I scanned the stands frantically until I found his royal blue SDU hat. Strangely enough, he was sitting next to my parents. And he wasn't the only one. There were three other scouts crowding around them.

At the start of this game, I wouldn't have dreamed that anybody would be interested in me. By the car ride home, my parents were telling me that I should be expecting some phone calls from the three college coaches that had witnessed my blast at Blaine.

I tried to remain calm in response to the situation. But still I remained close to the phone every moment that I was in the house. Two days later, the phone finally rang. I lunged for it, "Hello," I said as I rolled over on my bed.

"Hello, is this Jimmy?" The voice sounded very official. I hoped that SDU had come calling.

"This is Jimmy," I said excitedly. I stood up from my bed and started walking in small circles around my room.

"Jimmy, this is George Horn. I'm the assistant baseball coach at Pacific College. It's nice to finally get a chance to speak with you." George who?

"Well, it's nice to talk with you too, sir." I wasn't sure how to react to this phone call. I didn't want to say too much, so I followed Coach Horn's lead.

"Well, Jimmy, I'm actually calling this afternoon because I am really impressed with your skills as a baseball player. That homer at Blaine field, I mean, wow! I've also seen your high school statistics and it seems like you're a player who really has come into his own recently." He paused for a moment, and I wasn't sure if I should speak or let him finish. He continued on, "You seem to be a prime example of a player who has simply slipped through the cracks, and I must tell you that I'm one of the people that missed you. The good news is, it's not too late. Your Mom told me the other day that you still haven't decided which college you'll be attending in the fall. Is that true?" I started to feel like someone was actually recruiting me.

"That is true. I still don't know where I'm going to school. I really want to play baseball in college but since no one was recruiting me, I was going to try and walk on at - " I stopped before mentioning SDU. "I was just gonna try and walk on someplace."

"Jimmy, Pacific always holds one scholarship a year

for a special case, a late bloomer. This year, you're our special case. The coaches at Pacific feel as though we have truly found a diamond in the rough, and if you're interested we'd like to offer you a scholarship to come and play baseball for us."

I could not believe that after everything, Pacific had offered me a scholarship. I wasn't sure what to say, and since Coach Horn was insistent that I not rush my decision, he gave me his phone number and told me to call him when I knew what I wanted to do. Coach Horn sounded like a great guy, and I was really pumped about the possibility of playing baseball and attending school at Pacific College.

So that was that. After hardly being noticed in four years, I was simply in the right place at the right time. My home run at Blaine Field had changed my life. Now I had a full scholarship offer from one of the top baseball programs in the country. I hung up the phone with Coach Horn and sunk back into my bed, feeling a tremendous sense of relief. I knew I was going to play college baseball, someplace.

I still wanted to go to school at SDU, but I had to accept the fact that they hadn't called or written me in over a year. I wanted to be a Shark, but more and more, I felt like SDU didn't want me. I decided the next day that I would call Coach Horn and accept the scholarship. I wanted to go to a school that wanted me. I was going to play baseball at Pacific. Everything had changed. Two days after my homer at Blaine, I was spending an entire night going through my SDU paraphernalia to see what needed to be thrown out. I never thought this day would come. I went through about a dozen old t-shirts that my grandpa had given me, a couple of hats, a windbreaker that didn't fit, and the old letter from Larry Diaz. I looked at the walls of my room and I knew I would have to replace all the SDU posters and pennants that had adorned them since I was a little kid. The royal blue and white of SDU would give way to the orange and green of the Pacific Dolphins. I was excited about the Pacific scholarship, but I was also sad that my dream of going to San Diego University had ended.

The next day, just before I was about to call Coach Horn and let him know that I would be attending Pacific, the phone rang again. This time, it was Coach Diaz. He apologized for taking so long to contact me. After a minute or two of "small talk," Coach Diaz assured me that there would be a spot for me on the SDU baseball team. But he didn't offer a scholarship. While Pacific kept one scholarship for "diamond in the rough" players, SDU did not. I told him that I would need a day or two to think about what I wanted to do.

I decided to visit both schools and find out which college was best for me. The next morning, I took a drive to the SDU campus in downtown San Diego, and a half-hour after I'd left my house, I was standing alone on the SDU field. I took a long walk around silent Freedom Field, noticing the sign on the scoreboard that read "18 time National Champions." I thought back to all the great ones who wore the royal blue and white for the Sharks. I thought about how much wearing those colors, and that SD hat would mean to my family and me. After about fifteen minutes of walking and thinking, I knew what I had to do. I had to get home to call Coach Horn. I had a chance to play baseball for the Sharks and I wouldn't be able to forgive myself if I didn't take full advantage of that opportunity. I never made that trip to Pacific. My mind was already set on SDU.

As soon as I got home, I went up to my room and found Coach Horn's phone number. "Horn," he said as he picked up the phone.

"Hi Coach, this is Jimmy Hanks."

"Hey Jimmy," he spoke enthusiastically.

I cut right to the chase. "Coach, I've reached my decision." My subdued tone probably told him that I had decided against Pacific. "I'm sorry, but I'm going to SDU after all. Thank you so much for the offer, but I think that this is the only decision for me."

"Don't be sorry, Jimmy. San Diego University's a great school. We've got a pretty good rivalry going with those guys. I wish you the best luck in the future, son. Maybe I'll see you in Topeka someday." Topeka, Kansas was the site of the College Championship Series.

I smiled. "Yeah, I'll be there."

He laughed a little, "Ok, good luck Jimmy."

After I hung up the phone, I called Larry Diaz and told him that I'd be at the first practice when school started. My Blaine Field home run opened the doors of SDU baseball, and I walked right through. On September 1, 1994, I arrived at San Diego University, a college freshman and a student athlete.

Chapter 7: "Digging a Hole"

After the man had finished taping my wrists together, he moved around the room methodically restraining the rest of his prisoners one by one. The duct tape being peeled off the roll again and again sounded like fingernails screeching across a chalkboard. With every tear of the tape, another pair of wrists were tied tightly together, and another prisoner was bound and helpless.

I was squirming around on the floor, in an effort to stretch my wrists and move my hands. I wanted to try to get some blood flowing. When the man had finished taping Leon, he threw the roll of duct tape onto the floor, and once again, the room was silent. We were waiting for something, only none of us knew what. I forced a cough and drew the stares of Kevin and Chad. I then looked toward the door for a second, contorting my body enough to see that the gunman was still guarding our only exit. There was no way out.

He had noticed me glaring at him, "Hey you! Put your head back down!" I immediately planted my face back into the carpet.

The other criminal took control, "All right, here comes the fun part. Put your ankles behind your back. Move quickly!" The guy by the door pulled out some plastic ties from a small leather bag that he'd brought with him. They were going to be used to lock our ankles together behind our backs.

There I was, face in the carpet, with my hands and feet behind my back. I couldn't move a muscle in my body. And *even if I could, the two men carrying guns would have the last word. I was rendered completely helpless. I only remembered feeling this way one other time in my life...*

My freshman year at SDU was a roller-coaster ride. School was hard at first, but by the time baseball came around, I had my study habits down. I knew that even though baseball was my dream, nothing was as important as my education. Though I was weary of being cut, tryouts were pretty straightforward. Making the team wasn't a problem, playing time was.

This team was stacked. I remember the first day of practice. My head was on a swivel. These guys were hitting absolute bombs! They threw the ball harder than I'd ever seen, and their fielding abilities were phenomenal. One All-American after another took batting practice, and I stood with my mouth open, wondering if I had gotten in over my head. As I stretched out by the third base line, getting ready for my chance at-bat, I glanced around the field in awe. There was Jeff Jenson, a future Major League star for San Francisco, Pete Jacquez, now a starter for Toronto, and a bunch of other guys that are still chasing their dreams on Minor League fields across the country. Seth Ennis, an eventual starting pitcher for Pittsburgh, threw next to me, and his stuff was flat-out nasty. Could I hit those pitches? Jeff Jenson smashed another ball fifty feet over the center field wall. Could I even hit the ball that far? I learned during my first minutes of practice why SDU had not recruited me. They had plenty of guys just as good as me, if not better.

I had taken a long and bumpy road to SDU, getting there by the skin of my teeth. So when I finally stepped onto

Freedom Field in my Sharks practice jersey, I sighed with relief and accomplishment. An instant later, a rifled line drive came off the bat of Pete Jacquez right into my mitt at third base. The glove nearly flew off my fingers, and the burning sensation of the screaming liner hitting my hand made me flinch. I had been rudely awakened from enjoying my moment.

Throughout my freshman year, I played behind Ben Sutton, a freshman, who was given a full scholarship to backup senior Jose Alvara. Ben was being groomed to eventually take over the starting duties at third base. And let me tell you, being the backup to a backup was a humbling experience.

Ben was the third baseman of the future, and anyone else who thought about playing third would probably just back him up. I was that guy, a second-stringer. But still, I kept the faith that eventually I would be the Sharks starting third baseman.

Although I didn't play much, Coach was putting me in some crucial situations and I was responding. Everything was going pretty well until about a month into the season. The team was scheduled to go to Hawaii to play in a tournament. Only twenty-two players would be going to the island paradise, and I figured I would be one of the lucky ones. On the day Coach Jessup posted the list, I got up at 7:00 a.m., threw on a pair of old sweats, and jumped onto my bicycle, peddling down to Freedom Field as fast as I could. My dorm room was only about a three-minute bike ride from the field, but I got there in about half the time that morning. I threw down my bike in front of a short fence on the third base side, and jumped over it easily. I sprinted into the dugout, struggling to catch my breath.

The dugout led directly into our locker room, where Coach Jessup's office was located. I jogged through the corridors and couldn't help but think about all the great players who'd walked through these same hallways years before me. I wondered if one day, some freshman would think, "Hey, these were the same hallways that Jimmy Hanks walked through." That thought made me smile.

The clubhouse was dead silent. Every movement I made echoed off the empty lockers. After I opened up the heavy door to get into Coach Jessup's office, I noticed a white piece of paper pinned onto his bulletin board. I gingerly walked over to the list. I peered at the top of the alphabetical list and, using my finger as a marker, worked my way down. Alvara, Barone, my eyes continued down the list, one name at a time. Then I saw Henson. His name should have been after Hanks, but there *was* no Hanks. Maybe Coach spelled my name wrong. I checked through all the H's again, then all the way down the list one more time. My heart sunk. I hadn't made the travelling team.

I left Coach's office and went into the locker room to reflect. I needed a second to think things over. As I sat on the cold bench that morning, everything came crashing down on me. I had given up a full scholarship at Pacific to be a third stringer at SDU. I was a nobody. I'd slipped through the cracks again. Only this time, I thought something had to be said.

Practice was at 3:00 p.m. the next day, but I entered the opened door to Coach Jessup's office at 2:15. When he saw me come into the room, he took off his round-rimmed glasses and peered up at me. Coach always taught us to look people in the eye when we spoke to them. More importantly, he taught us to have a passion. He said that if you are passionate about what you do, you'll get to the "Majors" in every facet of life. By coming to his office, I intended to show him how passionate I was about the game of baseball.

"What can I do for you, Jimmy?" he asked.

I was nervous. Although Coach Jessup only stood about six feet tall and could be described as mild-mannered, his presence was larger than life. He intimidated me like no one else could. "Coach, I wanted to tell you about what's been going through my mind the past two days," I said meekly.

"Speak up, Jimmy," Coach said sternly.

I tried to talk a little louder. "I think I can play baseball. I really believe in my abilities, and I'm sure I'll be a good college player. What I'm trying to say is that, well, not making the traveling team really hurt me and - "

"Jimmy," Coach wasn't going to hear me out. Maybe I'd made a terrible decision by expressing my frustration to him.

He continued. "I also think you're a good player and I have no doubt that you're going to play for us in the future. It just so happens that we are loaded with talent on the left side of the infield this year, and it's not easy to find a spot for you. But I think that over time, that issue will resolve itself. Right now, I simply don't have enough spots on the field for all of you." This was not what I came to hear. "However, I do believe that you deserve to be making the trip to Hawaii. After I put up the roster, I reconsidered, and I've added your name to the new list." Now *that* was what I came to hear.

I could feel my face turning bright red. I'd come into his office to get a spot on the traveling team, and as it turned out, I already had one. I was stunned, a little embarrassed, but mostly just excited. I jumped out of my seat and stretched over to shake Coach's hand. "Thank you, Coach. Thank you so much. I promise I won't let you down," I was acting like a lunatic.

"You're welcome," he smiled. "Anything else?"

"No. Um … Aloha," I didn't care whether or not I set foot on that field in Hawaii. I was just happy to be a part of the team.

In the first game against Hawaii State, Jose Alvara opened at shortstop and Ben Barone started at third. I figured my only chance at any action would be as a defensive replacement late in the game. Or so I thought.

In the second inning, Ben Barone was hit by an inside fastball and was forced to leave the game for x-rays. I thought Coach would call on me to fill in for Barone, but instead, Ryan Gilbert was given the nod. I got a little more comfy in my seat at the end of the bench, thinking I wouldn't be moving any time soon. Strangely enough, in the fifth inning, Jose Alvara began clutching his hamstring in terrible pain, as he tried to leg out an infield hit. I could hear his howling from the dugout. There was no doubt that his day was over. Two starters on the left side of our infield had been injured. I decided I was done being passive about my role on the team. Someone needed to stand up. So *I* did.

Coach Jessup looked down the dugout, searching for a replacement. Finally he made eye contact with me. "Jimmy, get warmed up, you're in for Alvara."

No balls were hit to me in the fifth or the sixth inning, and in the top of the seventh, I tattooed a slider over the left field wall for my first collegiate home run. After I added a base-hit in the ninth, my imagination started running wild. I thought that if I played well in the second game of the double-header, I might be able to win a starting spot while Alvara and Barone were injured. But in thinking about the future, I lost focus on the present.

In the second game of the double-header, I started at shortstop. My first start in college. Everything seemed routine until the bottom half of the fourth. With a runner on first, and one out in a tie game, a laser was hit right at me. On contact, I began thinking, "Double play, double play." As I bent down to snag the grounder and flip it toward second base, the ball shot up and hit me square in the chest. An unlucky bounce, but an error, nonetheless.

I hoped that I'd have a chance to redeem myself. On the very next pitch, I did. A soft roller was tapped my way. I charged the ball, ready to make up for my error on the previous play. I knew I'd have to hurry if I was going to get the runner. As I bent over to pick up the trickling grounder, I looked up at the runners, and the ball scooted past me into left field. The lead runner scored from second and the Hawaii State fans began to jeer at me. I punched the center of my mitt in frustration. "Come on Jimmy, stay focused."

I tried to concentrate on the next batter, but my eyes kept wandering around the field. I saw Coach Jessup pacing in our dugout like he was about to break something. Our pitcher, Rudy Flowers, fired the rosin bag onto the back of the mound in disgust. Even Will Russell, our normally mild-mannered second baseman, was kicking up dirt near the bag at second.

Rudy then proceeded to walk the next batter on four straight pitches to load the bases. Coach motioned for the infield to play in on the grass. We were already down by one, and the drawn-in infield meant that we had to try and cut down the run at home. I dug my spikes into the grass, and I couldn't help thinking that I wanted the batter to hit the baseball to someone else. I had lost my confidence, and for the first time, I felt helpless on a baseball field. Strikeout, bunt, hit a fly ball, anything, just don't hit it to me.

Sure enough, just as I finished my thoughts, the Hawaii State batter hit a 2-1 pitch right up the middle. It was a semi-high chopper, and even in my fragile state of mind, I knew that this was an easy play. I fielded the ball cleanly, and quickly positioned myself for the throw, as State's speedy Mike Stein sprinted toward the plate. I threw a bullet that beat him by at least a step. The problem was, the ball flew five feet over our catcher's head and hit the backstop on a fly. All the runners were safe, and again I was the reason why.

We had fallen behind by two runs. We were the sixth ranked team in the country and were not supposed to lose to teams like Hawaii State. I shouldered the responsibility of the entire debacle. I had never been so embarrassed in my life. I felt like digging a hole in the ground at shortstop so I could hide myself from the rest of the world. The truth was, my three errors had already dug a hole for me.

The State fans continued hooting and hollering. "Shortstop, you're terrible, man! We should put you in a Hawaii State jersey, you're our best player." They hazed me unmercifully, and there was nothing I could do but stand there and take the harassment. I glanced into our dugout and watched a frustrated Coach Jessup kick over a bunch of bats that were leaned against the wall. I had never seen him so irate. The bats crashed to the ground and some of the players scrambled for a new location so they wouldn't get hit. Before the trip I told Coach Jessup that I wouldn't let him down. But my actions had spoken louder than my words. As I watched his tirade, I knew I hadn't made good on my promise.

Fortunately, Rudy was able to strike out the next batter on some great off speed stuff. We had finally recorded our second out. I could see the escape in front of me. I desperately wanted to get back into that dugout and out of the spotlight.

The next batter swung at an outside fastball, and barely caught the top of the pitch. I should have known. Once again, the ball was hit to me. I was scared out of my mind. I shuffled to the left and put my glove down just low enough for the ball to ricochet off the leather and into left field. My fourth error in the same inning! This had to be some sort of record. Two runs scored on that play and Hawaii State went ahead by four.

Coach Jessup had seen enough. After that error, he

pulled me out of the game. Our right fielder, Jeff Jenson, who had never played the infield before, came in to play shortstop. Pitchers were supposed to be changed in the middle of innings, not shortstops. But I was so putrid that I'd left Coach with no other option. I wondered if and when he'd give me the chance to dig myself out of the hole I dug in Hawaii.

As I jogged off the field, the opposing fans stood and clapped. Their sarcastic cheering and laughter was the loudest ovation ever directed at me. Coach glared at me from the top step of the dugout. His patience had to be wearing thin.

Chapter 8: "The Wrong Side of the Fence"

The men had finished taping everyone's ankles together. I knew this because the sound of the tape being unraveled had ceased, if only for a moment. With the exception of the pizza guy, no one had interrupted this robbery. The hold-up was going exactly as the two criminals had planned and I sensed that they could have fled the scene at any time. But they didn't and I was left wondering why.

As the pain intensified in my wrists and ankles, I began to accept the fact that today was going to be my last day on earth. If the criminals wanted us dead, we were going to be shot. But why would they want us dead? How could anyone, under any circumstance, kill another human being?

Just as these questions raced through my head, I noticed Kevin and Chad making eye contact with me from across the floor. One of the gunmen had left the room to search the house for valuables and we were left with just one guard. Kevin and Chad were signaling me with wide eyes, motioning their heads toward the lone gunman. I guessed my teammates thought that this was our last chance at a daring escape. Just as I was trying to figure out what they were trying to tell me, Kevin jumped to his feet with Chad following close behind. They bull-charged the gunman, knocking him to the ground.

His gun hit the floor with a thump and everyone began to wiggle and fight in a desperate attempt to seize the weapon. I rose to my feet, and scrambled toward the pile. The problem was, having our hands tied behind our backs gave us a distinct disadvantage in the fight for the loose gun. Just as I reached for the fumbled pistol and placed my hand on it, the man with the green bandanas came storming into the room. He brutally kicked me in the stomach, knocking me backward. He then grabbed the gun from my hand. If I wouldn't have been tied up, I may have been able to hold onto it. In a frightening moment he pointed the gun directly at Kevin, "Back up! Everybody get back!" We all moved toward the floor again. Our attempt had failed. We were in some serious trouble.

Both gunmen were huffing and puffing with exhaustion, "We tried to do this the nice way, but you guys couldn't handle that." He tossed the duct tape to his partner who lay on the floor with a bloody lip, "That's it, hog tie'em."

I knew what it was to be "hog-tied," and I knew we were in a lot of trouble. I must have seen some movie where there was a robbery and two guys were getting "hog-tied," but for the life of me I couldn't remember what the movie was. This actually bothered me. Either way, I knew that having my wrists tied to my ankles behind my back was uncomfortable.

Again, I was first in the taping line-up. "This is going to hurt," the man said chuckling under his breath as he bent down to tape me. He yanked on my wrists until they were touching my ankles behind my back. It was the most physical pain I had ever endured. I moved my body around to try and reach a spot of comfort, but failed to. The man would not stand for my movement, he waved his gun at me, "Don't you move," he said harshly as he stomped his foot into my back, a punish-

ment for my squirming and our failed escape attempt.

He wrapped the tape around the balls of my feet and the middle of my hands, three times. In that moment of sheer humiliation, pain, and suffering, when I felt like my life was slowly being taken from me, I remembered that I had felt pain before. Only then, my ego was badly bruised, not my wrists and ankles. And the culprit wasn't a hardened criminal, but one of the great people I've met in my life, Coach Mark Jessup. I closed my eyes, leaned my eyelids hard against the carpet, and I could picture him standing in front of me. In that moment, I remembered how badly I'd been hurt during my freshman season...

As the playoffs neared and the regular season concluded, our team was rolling. But I had little to do with the success. Nonetheless, as the season progressed, Coach started to put me in the field for the last few innings of some games. I only made one other error during my freshman year, and I earned back the reputation of being a solid fielder, even after Hawaii.

Still, I suffered through a long season. Only twenty-two players traveled to the conference games and I felt like I deserved one of those spots. But every week when the roster was posted, there was no "Hanks" on the list. So while the team made road trips all over the country, I was left alone. Usually, I would go home for the weekend and hang out with my family. I always liked being home, but my family knew my heart was someplace else. I wanted to be on the road. I wanted to be one of the guys.

The Monday practice after a weekend road trip was always the worst for me. The guys would talk about the big hit that won the game, or how a strong pitching performance got us another victory. They would be laughing about some funny story that happened during the weekend, and I would just sit there and listen, laughing when they laughed, and smiling when I saw someone look over at me.

I had nothing to say to anyone. What could I say? They didn't want to hear about the bacon double cheeseburger that Mom made me on Saturday night, or how Shawn and I went surfing and thought we saw a shark. So I sat quietly on those days, and week after week, my insides were torn apart. Every Monday I was reminded of my role on this team. I was a practice player. Sure, I would put on a uniform for home games, maybe I'd even play an inning or two, but most times I would just sit there and gather splinters on the bench. My freshman year was a time when I really improved on chewing sunflower seeds and drinking Gatorade.

At least the team was playing great. Our first-place finish in the South Pacific Conference assured us of a post-season berth. The fact that we were winning kept me doubly-motivated to work my way onto the post-season roster. If I could do that, I would have a chance to reach the College Championship Series.

The College Championship Series is played in Topeka, Kansas every June. Most teams never have a shot to reach America's heartland. Coming into my freshman year, SDU had not been to the College Championship Series in twelve years.

The 1995 Sharks were different, though. I knew that I would probably only have one opportunity to reach Topeka during my college career, and I thought this was that chance. So I kept working hard. I got some hits here and there, and my average crept up to around .270 for the season. I was finally making some progress.

I thought that the strides I had made would earn me a spot on the playoff roster. In the playoffs, three additional slots were added for back-ups. This would assuredly benefit me. I was confident that I would be one of the twenty-five players on the roster. I had to be. Who else would Coach take? I was Ben Barone's backup, but his wrist had been bothering him all year long. In all likelihood, he would be unable to participate in the playoffs and I would take his place.

We finished the regular season with a record of 46-14. On the Thursday after our last game, we would leave San Diego to start on our road to college baseball's "grandest stage," Topeka, Kansas. First, we would have to survive a four-team regional playoff to earn an invitation.

Coach told us he would post the twenty-five man playoff roster on Tuesday after practice. I had grown accustomed to the Tuesday postings during the season, and the disappointment that came along with the white piece of paper that never had the name "Hanks" on it. With three extra spots, I was sure this Tuesday would be different.

Our practice ended and before we were allowed to see the roster, Coach called us together for a meeting. We all took a knee and circled around him on the grass in left field. Most of us were still huffing and puffing from the sprints that customarily concluded practice.

Coach smiled and then turned serious, putting his hand in front of his face to contend with the southern California sun. "While you guys catch your breath, I want to congratulate you all on an amazing regular season. I am very proud of the heart each one of you has shown throughout." Everyone else smiled for a second. I just stared at Coach, looking for clues as to who was going to the playoffs and who was going home. He continued. "If we can show that kind of heart in the playoffs, then I believe we'll be this year's National Champions."

All of the guys were getting a little excited and started grumbling. Coach cut us off. "But first, we have to reach Topeka. And as many of you guys already know, that's the toughest part. That being said, on Thursday the team bus will leave at 2:00 p.m. sharp for Sacramento and the West regional."

We all started clapping. Most of the guys spoke about how we could beat Sacramento State, and I did the same. As more of the guys shook my hand, and looked into my eyes with the same excitement I was feeling, I realized that I *was* part of this team.

Coach Jessup had momentarily lost control of his meeting. He quickly brought us back to reality. "All right, enough. Let's celebrate when we win the whole thing." He spoke powerfully. "I have an announcement to make concerning the roster for the playoffs." Everyone became silent. My heart skipped a beat. Coach cleared his throat and continued, "I'm going to use the same roster for Sacramento and Topeka. I've decided to go with the usual twenty-two that we traveled with all season. You guys know who you are."

That group did not include me, but I still had a chance. The moment of truth was only seconds away. What about the other three spots? "I'm going with one extra catcher, and two extra pitchers. I spoke to the three of you guys and you also know who you are." I'd been cut again.

He went on for a minute about how the two pitchers and the catcher would be of the most use in case of injuries. He said we had enough backups in terms of position players, and he apologized to everyone who wasn't making the trip. I felt like he was speaking directly to me. I was absolutely devastated.

The team would practice on Wednesday and Thursday, and Coach said that the guys who were not on the twenty-five-man roster were free to go home for the summer. As each player came to console me, I remember having a very hard time comprehending what had happened. All the while, I struggled to fight back tears. I had come to SDU to play baseball, not to go home while the team played on. I wanted to tell Coach Jessup that. I yelled out to him as he passed the pitcher's mound.

"Coach," I said loudly. He turned his head, startled, and walked back toward me. Our eyes didn't meet until we stood next to one another.

He put his arm on my shoulder. "Jimmy?"

I wasn't sure why I'd called out to him, but I knew I had to say something. "Coach, I was wondering if it would be all right with you if I continued to practice with the team for the next two days?"

Coach patted me on the back, "Sounds good. I'll see you at practice tomorrow. And don't worry so much, you're only a freshman, you've got three more shots at this."

I practiced in agony for the next two days, and at 2:00 on Thursday afternoon, the bus to Sacramento pulled up to Freedom Field. I stood by the bus that afternoon and said goodbye to every player and coach headed to the regional. I wished them luck and told them that I believed they would win the whole thing.

The bus revved its engine and slowly moved out of the parking lot. I watched the fading caravan for as long as I could, hoping for some miracle, hoping for a flat tire, hoping that the bus would turn around and Coach would ask me to come along. There was no such luck. Twenty-five of my teammates, twenty-five of my best friends pulled away that afternoon in search of their dreams. A few minutes later, I pulled away in my lonely pick-up truck and drove home to Oceantown in search of my lost baseball career.

I settled in at home, got out my surfboard, and started my summer vacation. Mom and Dad were proud because I earned a perfect 4.0 in school that semester for the first time in college. I was happy too. My good grades gave me career options beyond baseball.

Still, I couldn't stop thinking about the team. I followed them every step of the way on the internet and in the papers. They were steam rolling through the regional and with each victory, the guys moved a little closer to Topeka.

The morning after the final game in Sacramento, I set my alarm for 6:00 a.m. I could hardly sleep that night because I was so nervous about the team's results. When the alarm clock shouted, I jumped out of bed, ran down the steps, and out the front door. I opened the newspaper and threw everything but the sports page to the concrete. The headline was right there, "At Last! Sharks Headed Back to Topeka!" The guys had done it, they were headed to Topeka. Despite not being there with them, I shared in their excitement.

Later that night, I started to reflect on my missed opportunity. The team was going to Topeka, and I was going downstairs to dinner. I was silent at the table that night. I couldn't really eat and just stared into my food. Then, as if from nowhere, my mother said the strangest thing to me, "Jimmy?"

"Yes, mom?" I looked away from my mashed potatoes.

"Do you want to drive to Topeka?" Mom asked.

"What are you talking about?" I said, wondering if I was hearing things.

"I said, do you want to drive to Topeka?"

I looked over at Dad. He shrugged his shoulders and smiled. Obviously he was in on this plan as well. "Drive to Topeka? Are you two crazy?" I thought they were both losing their minds. Maybe they'd overdosed on broccoli or something.

"I'm serious, let's go. You and me, it'll be fun." Mom started to laugh a little.

As I raked my fork through my mashed potatoes, making them look like a baseball diamond, I thought about her suggestion. Drive to Topeka, see the guys, go to the College Championship Series, my mind was made up. "If you're serious, I'm already in the car."

After dinner that night, we mapped out our trip and packed our stuff into her Jeep. Mom and I left early the next morning for a three-day drive to Topeka, which would have us arriving the night before our first game. Mom had saved the day.

Four mornings later, we entered the ballpark around 8:45 a.m. I walked around the stadium so I could see the names of all the Major Leaguers who'd played in Topeka. Rockport Stadium had hosted some amazing games. I walked around and began to feel the mystique of the College Championship Series. I made my way past the ushers and down the steps to the edge of the SDU dugout. I stood and watched the guys talk to one another, toss the baseball, and chew on seeds. Finally, I caught the eye of Jose Alvara.

"Hey," I shouted to him in the dugout.

Jose looked at me and pointed, "Hanks!" Suddenly the entire bench exploded. The guys started running over to make sure their eyes weren't deceiving them. They formed a line in front of me, and one by one, each of them shook my hand or gave me a hug. They thanked me for coming all the way to Topeka to support them. It was one of the greatest moments of my life. For those ten minutes, I was a part of the team again, even though I was standing on the wrong side of the fence.

Ben Barone was one of the first to come over to me. "Jimmy, you deserve to be in that dugout with us." He had never said anything to me about the fact that he was the one on the traveling team and I was left off. "I think it is so great that you came all the way to Topeka."

My response to him was more of a question, "What's it like, Ben?"

He looked around at the field for a second, "It's awesome, Jim." He shook my hand and walked back to the dugout.

Coach Jessup was the last one to come over and say hello to me. "You really amaze me, kid. It is great to see you here. If you want to come and sit on the bench with your teammates, you're more than welcome."

The guys made me feel welcome on the bench, even though I was wearing street clothes. I'd usually rotate between a seat next to Mom in the stands, and a seat in the dugout with the guys. I sat in my blue jeans and my SDU hat, and cheered loudly as they advanced to the final game of the College Championship Series. During those five games, I decided that no matter what happened during the Series, I wouldn't step between the lines of Rockport Field. I wasn't there as a player. I didn't belong on that field.

The championship game was against our biggest rival, Pacific. As the guys took batting practice that day, I walked around the back of the cage. I watched the teams get ready for the biggest game of their lives and I listened to the chatter between them. Most of the players from SDU and Pacific knew each other because they all grew up playing baseball in Southern California. I moved around the cage and spoke casually with some of the guys, but I made sure never to touch fair territory.

I was walking behind the cages when I recognized an old friend of mine, Pacific's assistant coach, George Horn. This was the same Coach Horn who had watched me play at Blaine Field a year earlier, and the same Coach Horn who had offered me a scholarship to play baseball for Pacific.

I walked over to him. He was propped up against the batting cage, mesmerized by the "pinging" of the aluminum bats. "Coach Horn," I called out to him.

He looked in my direction, "Jimmy Hanks, how are you?"

The last time I talked to him was when I decided to go to SDU instead of Pacific. "I could be better." I pointed to my outfit, making him aware of the fact that I had not been asked to wear a uniform for the game. "But I'm not complaining, just happy to be here."

"How'd your season go?" He asked.

"Some ups and some downs. A few hits, a few errors. I'm just hoping that I get a chance to be a full time starter next year," I really thought that was a possibility.

"You'll get your chance, be patient, you're a good ballplayer."

"Thanks, Coach."

Coach Horn smiled, "And what did I tell you? Didn't I guarantee that Pacific would be here once during your four years?" He had made good on his guarantee and I couldn't help but wonder what would have happened if I went to Pacific instead of SDU. If I would have said "yes" to Coach Horn that day in his office, I might have had a uniform on that afternoon, instead of a windbreaker.

We said goodbye and Coach Horn wished me luck in the future. I walked behind the batting cages again and made my way down the third base line. I looked at the chalk that separated the playing field from foul territory. My teammate, Brendan Hershey came from behind me and tossed me a mitt, "Hey, Jim, you want to have a catch?"

I looked at the chalked lines again. "Nah, I'm fine. I'm going to stay over here, you know." I wasn't going to step onto that field.

Brendan nodded his head. He understood and decided not to force the issue. I peered out at the freshly cut grass, and the perfectly raked infield dirt, and I made a pact with myself. I would do everything in my power to get back to Topeka, as a player. Then I would be able to walk onto that field with my head held high and a Sharks uniform on my back.

The final score that day was 11-5. Pacific College dominated us from the get go, and they were crowned 1995 Champions. Before I left the field, I threw some dirt from behind the batting cage into my pocket. I wanted to take a small piece of Rockport Field with me. When I got home, I put that piece of Topeka into a small envelope. One day, I hoped to return that dirt to the field I took it from.

Chapter 9: "It's Just a Game"

Wrapped in a ball of duct tape, with my face burning against the rugged carpet, and my mind racing in a thousand different directions, I could sense the end of this fiasco rapidly approaching. I heard the tape being unraveled again. We had already been "hog-tied," where were they going to put more tape?

Then I realized that the tape had to be going over our mouths, to ensure that we stayed quiet. I began licking my lips in a panic. I don't know what triggered that response. I guess I didn't want to die from suffocation. I knew that the tape wouldn't stick to my saliva, so over and over, I frantically licked my lips...

When I came back to SDU for my sophomore season, I was really licking my lips. I had a fresh start ahead of me and was determined to make my career a success. I began lifting weights and running, deciding that the best way to erase memories of my disappointing freshman year was to have a memorable sophomore one.

In the off-season, Jose Alvara, last year's starting shortstop, signed a contract with San Diego. Ben Barone had graduated, leaving Ryan Gilbert, Ernie Cilla and me, as the only three guys on the team who could play the left side of the infield. I knew Ryan was probably going to be the starting shortstop, and although Ernie was a good ballplayer, I was sure that if I practiced hard, third base would be my position.

About five weeks before our first practice, I had a conversation with Ryan Gilbert that turned all my plans upside down. Ryan and I sat next to each other in accounting class. We were good friends, though our talks never strayed far from baseball. We began discussing the upcoming season as we waited for the professor to arrive. I told him that I believed he'd be our starting shortstop, and I'd be the starting third baseman, in our first game against Upper Nevada.

He quickly ended my dreams. "I guess you didn't hear, huh?"

"Hear what?" Our professor arrived and Ryan looked straight ahead, ending our conversation. But I had to know what he was talking about. "What? Heard what, Ryan?" I was whispering so I wouldn't disrupt class.

He whispered back trying not to draw any attention to himself. "We signed a shortstop yesterday."

Oh no, I thought. Ryan continued, "He was a freshman All-American two years ago. Desmond Samuel, a transfer from Trenton College, you ever heard of him?"

I had heard of him, and I knew he was a great ballplayer. Part of me was excited because we were getting another excellent player on our team, but another part of me was crushed because I was staring another season of bench warming right in the face. "Are you kidding me?" I asked.

Ryan shook his head. He wasn't kidding. Samuel would most definitely be our starting shortstop and I was destined to be the odd man out again. This meant that Ernie, Ryan and I would compete for playing time at third base. Just when my window of opportunity looked wide open, Samuel came in and shut it in my face. Nothing at SDU was coming easy for me.

I showed up for practice on January 2nd, and upon arrival, the dogfight for the starting third base position began. Luckily, I was playing the best baseball of my entire life. Suddenly, my line drives were bullets, and I was hitting to all fields with power. I had no idea what happened. Something just clicked, I guess.

Just two days before our first game, Ernie Cilla was painfully eliminated from the competition for the starting spot. He was hit by a tailing fastball that broke his arm in two places. I felt terrible for Ernie, but I knew that his injury meant that either Ryan or I would be the Sharks starting third baseman.

When our first game against Upper Nevada finally arrived, I was excited. I anticipated finally seeing my name in the starting line-up. But when I checked the card, I received the same old news. Ryan Gilbert was penciled in as the starting third baseman. I started my sophomore season in a familiar seat, on the bench. I was angry. What would I have to do to earn Coach Jessup's respect? I sat through the entire first game wondering.

The game was close and Coach began to pace around the dugout. He noticed me moping at the end of the bench. He knew that I was upset. I radiated frustration. "Hanks, get over here," he demanded. Seth Ennis moved away from Coach, leaving an open seat next to him. I sat down. He didn't look happy with me, and spoke harshly. "I want you to stop your pouting and be a man. You're not helping this team by sitting in the dugout with a long face. Shape up! This is supposed to be fun.

Now grab a helmet, you're pinch hitting for Gilbert."

When I came to the plate in the seventh inning, a familiar face was there to greet me on the pitcher's mound. Josh Green. Josh had played his high school baseball at East High School in San Diego, and I had faced him a number of times before. Seeing him eased my nerves a bit as I dug in for the first at-bat of my sophomore season.

Coach had given me a chance, and I had to do something to prove that I deserved to be on that field. After working the count full, I swung at a change-up and connected. The ball cleared the right field fence before I could get halfway down the first base line. I hadn't swung that hard, but the pitch hit the fat part of the bat and I used my legs to lift the ball right out of the park. I wanted to pump my fists, but I didn't. I tried to act like I'd been in this situation before, though I couldn't remember the last time I came through with a hit that meant something.

That one hit changed everything for me. I started every game for the rest of my career as a Shark. Soon enough I was getting hits every day. Pete Jacquez and Jeff Engle, both current Major Leaguers, hit third and fourth. And there *I* was, the sophomore with no scholarship, the guy who no one believed in, hitting in the five hole and helping one of the best teams in the nation win ballgame after ballgame.

My sophomore year went great. I batted .342 with ten home runs, and helped our team win the Southern Pacific Conference for the second straight year. So when June rolled around, I began dreaming big again. I began dreaming of Topeka. But those dreams came crashing down when Cheyenne beat us twice in the regional, and crushed our title hopes. Another year had passed and I hadn't returned to the "promised land."

Individually, I was more than pleased with my sophomore season. I even began to think about the possibility of entering the Major League Draft after my junior year. Up until that year, I always thought that I would graduate from SDU and move back to Oceantown to become a banker, like my dad. That was my plan, and I had done everything academically that was necessary to achieve that goal. But after my unexpected sophomore explosion, a future in banking was the last thing I had in mind. Baseball was what I thought about as a career choice.

We were only two days away from the first game of my junior season, and I could hardly stand the anticipation. Before the madness began, I had a few minutes to relax. I was lying down in my apartment, reading Sports Illustrated, when a phone call jerked me out of bed.

"Jimmy?" the voice on the other end asked.

"Yeah," I said in a tired groan.

"You know who this is?"

I knew exactly who it was. That same voice had once convinced me that I was a baseball ballplayer.

"Nick Erickson, it's been a long time my friend." I was surprised to hear from my old high school buddy.

We did the regular introductory stuff that people do when they haven't spoken in a while, and about ten minutes later, we were both pretty much caught up on each other's lives.

When we had finished telling our stories, Nick offered me some other news. "Oh yeah, before I hang up, I was saving some great news for you." I could tell he was smiling on the other end.

"What news?" I asked excitedly.

"I was talking to this Milwaukee scout yesterday, and he asked me if I still kept in contact with you. I said that I did, and that we were still good friends. Anyway, he starts rambling about how he used to scout California, and how he saw us both play in high school. Then he says, now get this, he and his scouts have you projected as a first through fourth round pick in the upcoming draft. First through fourth! That's the big time, bro. I thought that you - "

I cut Nick off. "First through fourth? He really said that?"

"First through fourth." Nick repeated. I could hear the enthusiasm in his voice.

I took a moment to collect my breath and struggled to find words to keep a conversation going. I was too busy replaying the words, "first through fourth" over and over and over again in my head.

Nick had a parting shot before he hung up. "Hey, aren't you glad I told you baseball was your sport? You could be on some basketball court right now, waiting for a pick-up game." He laughed loudly.

"I'm just glad I listened. Thanks again, Nick." The conversation was over.

I hung up the phone and laid back down on my bed. I

was happy that I'd stuck with baseball.

My junior season was about to begin, and suddenly I was a hot commodity. Scouts from twenty-five of the thirty major league franchises had contacted me, and for the first time ever, I was being heavily recruited. If I were selected high enough in June's draft, I would probably forego my senior year of college to play minor league baseball. I couldn't help but get caught up in all the pre-draft hoopla.

I approached my junior season with a new brazen attitude. After all, I was a professional prospect. Having that cocky disposition turned out to be the worst mistake I ever made in the game of baseball. I began to put unbearable pressure on myself. This added tension had me swinging for home runs like I was Babe Ruth, but instead, I was striking out like Ruth Hanks, my great-grandma. In trying to impress everyone, I fell flat on my face.

I kept taking extra batting practice, but that didn't seem to work. I slept with my baseball bat, but still I couldn't hit. I changed my pre-game routine, and my post-game routine. I started eating chicken instead of pasta before the games, I even asked my brothers for help, but nothing could get me out of my slump. I was hitting a measly .198 through the first twenty games of my junior season. If I had any aspirations of playing baseball beyond college, I knew that I would have to step up my game, and quickly.

We had already finished one-third of the season and though I was still hitting fourth in the lineup, my lack of productivity was killing the team. Finally, some advice from an old friend alleviated some of my anxieties. Just before we were ready to do battle in the desert heat at the University of Phoenix, I heard a familiar sound at the water fountain behind our dugout.

"Hey, Hanks," a deep husky voice called out to me from a close distance.

I turned around and saw Roger Davie standing before me. We talked for the next few minutes about what was happening to me on the baseball field. Roger had noticed a decline in my numbers, and he asked me what the problem was. I started to talk about my hands being slow, how I was taking my eye off the ball, and pressing for base hits. He cut me off.

"That's all bull and you know it. First of all, what happened to the happy-go-lucky kid that I knew in high school? You're too serious Hanks…bat speed, and your eyes. If you want to succeed in the game of baseball, you have to play the game because you love it. You have to have that passion. It sounds to me like you're more concerned with being a high draft-pick than a great ballplayer. Keep it simple, like when you were a kid. See the ball, and hit it, field the ball and throw it. It's just a game, Jimmy. Don't ever let this great *game* turn into a business. Now let me see that high school smile."

I smiled for Roger, and it was an authentic one. He was absolutely right. In the rat race to be a high draft-pick, I'd forgotten how much I loved playing the game of baseball. I loved the one-on-one showdown between the batter and the pitcher, the smell of fresh oil in my glove, and the look of my dirtied, brown uniform after a nine inning battle. I loved hearing the sound of a collision at home plate. I loved the helmet slaps and the baseball jive in the dugout. A million more memories came to my mind. I could picture the great plays and the awful ones. I missed *playing* the game. I needed to relax and have fun again. I shook Roger's hand. A weight had been lifted from my shoulders.

Ryan Gilbert saw me grinning when I came back into the dugout. "What the heck are you so happy about?" he asked.

I looked at Ryan, still smiling. "I'm back," I told him. And I was.

I did what Roger had told me. I saw the ball and I hit it, attacking the first pitch thrown to me. The result was a homerun. The baseball landed some forty feet beyond the fence in left field, and the usually raucous University of Phoenix crowd became completely silent. I'd finally broken out of the worst slump of my life. As I crossed home plate, I looked above our dugout, and there was Roger Davie. He nodded his head in approval. I nodded back.

I ended up hitting ten home runs in the last forty games of that season and my batting average shot up over one hundred points. I had refocused myself and my concerns were no longer affiliated with the draft. I simply wanted to win. And we did win, forty-five times to be exact. But our season ended with a heart-wrenching 9-8 loss to Birmingham in the playoffs.

On the plane ride home from Alabama, all I could think about was how I had failed to achieve my goal of reaching Topeka. I sat back and watched as the plane soared through the clouds and over the Rocky Mountains. I was in my own world. I stared into oblivion, wondering if my career as a Shark was over. Then Bryan Vogelsong, my best friend on the team, tapped me on the shoulder. "So is that it?" I had been asking myself that exact same question for the entire flight. After all my dreaming about wearing the royal blue and white at SDU, could I give up my last year in a Shark uniform? Was I really ready for life in the Minor Leagues, a life away from my family and friends? Was I prepared to give up my last chance to reach Topeka?

Bryan repeated his question, "Jimmy, is that it? Are you done?"

"Is what it?" I turned to face him, buying time by repeating his question.

"Was that the last time we'll ever see Jimmy Hanks at third base for the Sharks?" Bryan took a sip of his orange juice and looked at me. I stared off in the opposite direction, unable to answer.

Chapter 10: "Getting Up"

The shorter and stockier of the criminals slapped two pieces of tape over my mouth in a careless fashion. The tape barely stuck to my wet lips. If I hadn't been licking them, I wouldn't have been able to breathe at all.

The man circled the room in the same manner that he did when he tied us up. The hold-up had gone on for close to an hour now, and everyone had grown tired of being afraid. We were simply exhausted. Each person stared off into space, and feet that were shaking a few minutes earlier were now lifeless, blanketed in sticky tape.

My entire body was now completely numb. The only good news was that the pain momentarily subsided, and the numbness I felt was almost comforting. My time on this earth was nearly expired, and being numb brought me that much closer to the feeling of death.

I noticed that the guy who had been watching the door went into the bedrooms, and grabbed all the sheets and blankets from the beds. He threw a heavy brown blanket over the top of me. But he did a poor job of hiding my face, and when I shook a little, I was exposed. As soon as the man saw this, he palmed my head like a basketball and forcefully pushed it under the blanket. He then adjusted the covers, completely covering my face. My world was dark again.

From beneath the blankets, I heard the voices of the two gunmen just a few feet away. "Let's do it now." I recognized the husky voice to be the man in the black ski mask. He was in charge, and so far, whatever orders he commanded went uncontested by his partner.

"You better get the car started then. We're gonna have to get out of here in a hurry after the neighbors hear the gunshots." The man with the green bandanas replied.

A chill ran down my spine. I was about to be shot and killed. The men didn't want to see the faces of their victims when they fired the bullets. It was much easier to shoot a pile of blankets, than to look a human being in the eye and pull the trigger.

I refused to let them take the easy way out. I began to squirm around, trying to push my face out from underneath the covers. If the men were going to shoot me, they would have to look me directly in the eyes. I was ready to die, but I refused to do it beneath a blanket. My parents had always taught me to face my problems, not to turn and run. And in the final moments of my life, I was determined to look death in the face.

Struggling to get out from beneath the covers, I shifted and pushed until I could see the light of the room a few inches away. It was the hardest struggle that I'd ever fought. My body was numb and tired, but I continued to push my face against what felt like miles of brown blanket.

I remembered the last time I'd faced an uphill battle. I remember the last time a blanket had been thrown over me. Only then, it was my baseball career that was about to be shot...

It was day two of the Major League Baseball Draft, and the Hanks house was silent. Mom and Dad were at work, and my brothers were out surfing or playing soccer. Everyone knew that I needed to be alone that day. The first day of the draft had come and gone, and I had not been selected. I sat reading a book to keep myself busy while I waited for the call of a scout.

On the first day of the draft, seven hundred and fifty players had been chosen. Three guys on my team were drafted in the top sixteen rounds. Seth Ennis and Rudy Flowers were selected in the ninth and tenth rounds, respectively, by St. Louis and New York. Desmond Samuel became a fifteenth round choice of Boston. Numerous scouts had told me that I would assuredly be the first player from my team to be selected, but while Rudy, Seth and Desmond could begin planning a future in baseball, I was left undrafted.

The phone kept ringing, but each time I thought my prayers had been answered, the call was for someone else. There was a call for Dave, a couple for Mom, and one from a telemarketing guy who I should have been a lot nicer to. All that talk about me being a "first through fourth" round selection, well, that was nothing more than talk. And as the morning turned into afternoon, on the draft's second day, the phone sat quietly next to me. I knew I was running out of time. It was five minutes to five when I finally gave up and tossed the portable phone onto the couch. I walked over to the computer and clicked onto the Major League Baseball web site. There was a message written in large, capital letters, "THE 1997 MAJOR LEAGUE DRAFT IS NOW OVER. FIFTEEN HUNDRED PLAYERS FROM HIGH SCHOOLS, JUNIOR COLLEGES, AND COLLEGES HAVE BEEN SELECTED BY THIRTY DIFFERENT FRANCHISES. MAJOR LEAGUE BASEBALL WISHES ALL OF THESE BALLPLAYERS THE BEST OF LUCK IN THEIR QUEST TO BECOME MAJOR

LEAGUERS." I had gone undrafted. Two days, fifty rounds, fifteen hundred players and no Jimmy Hanks.

I grabbed my keys from the table and stormed outside to my truck. I had to get out of my house. I didn't want to face the curious eyes of my brothers, or see the saddened look on my mother's face when I told her that I had not been selected. I was sure Dad would have some words of wisdom, but I didn't think they'd do me any good in my fragile state of mind. So I drove off, leaving the computer monitor on with the words still hanging in the air.

That day, I drove down streets that I'd been on my entire life, but something was suddenly strange. Something was wrong. I didn't know where I was going anymore. I was lost. Before that day, I was driving to be a baseball player. That dream was quickly crumbling before my eyes.

About an hour later, I ended up at Coastal Field. I didn't know what brought me here, but when I got out of my truck and walked down the steps towards the first base line, I knew there was no place I'd rather be. I always felt better when I stepped onto a baseball diamond and inside the chalked lines. Ironically, it was baseball that kept breaking my heart, again and again.

I walked around the field, and could tell right away that baseball was in season. The smeared chalk lines looked like they had recently been stepped on. I wondered if I had just missed a game. I had played on that field as a kid, so I knew there was a bench beyond the outfield fence. I made my way to the deepest part of the ballpark and climbed over the short fence that once seemed monstrous. I took a seat with a view of the Pacific Ocean.

There was no one in sight, and I leaned back, deep in thought. I watched the waves crash and splash below. The sun faded slowly in the background. I was in the middle of a beautiful postcard, and I knew it.

At that moment, I decided that the game of baseball was hurting me too much. For the first time ever, I actually thought about giving it up. I was sick and tired of having baseball kick my butt. I was tired of expectations that were never met. Besides, there were plenty of other things I could do. I had options because I was well educated. I was going to receive my college degree in less than a year. I thought back to my original plan of becoming a banker, and I wondered if I would ever be able to walk away from baseball. I turned this question over and over in my head.

But how could I walk away after all I'd been through? I started to recall all the tough times. I remembered sitting in my kitchen after getting cut from the Tidal Waves and, a few years later, walking through the double-doors of Bayside High School as "the new kid." I would never forget the angered expression on Tony Garrett's face when he ordered me to throw at Silvano. I could still see the image of Larry Diaz walking right passed me after my two home run game against Kingston. I heard the fans laughing in Hawaii, jeering at me after my four errors in one inning. I remembered sitting in the dugout in Topeka, wearing blue jeans, while my teammates fought for a Championship. I had gotten up each and every time I'd been knocked down before. "I can take more punches than you can." I've lived by those words. I could never quit.

I turned around and stared at the bases, and the pitcher's mound, and the outfield fence. I loved baseball more than I realized. I should have been fed up with going to baseball fields, with striking out, making errors, and missing chances. Instead, I drove an hour on the worst day of my baseball life to get back on the diamond. I wanted so badly to play the game I loved for a living. I would give every ounce of myself for the slim possibility that I could become a Major Leaguer. I would try so hard, if only I was given the chance.

I stood up from the bench, hopped over the fence and began walking towards the batter's box. Once I got there I asked the imaginary umpire for timeout. He granted me my wish and I adjusted my helmet as I dug in. I listened to the crowd roar at the empty field in the middle of nowhere. Suddenly, I had my favorite bat on my shoulder. I was wearing a San Diego uniform, and I noticed my name on the towering scoreboard in left field. "Now batting for San Diego, third baseman, number 30, Jimmy Hanks." I tipped my hat to the imaginary crowd, and checked the scoreboard. It was the World Series, game seven, two outs, bases loaded, we're down by three, bottom of the ninth. I'd been up in that situation a million times in my dreams. I stood in the batter's box and stared down an imaginary pitcher in front of me. He spit onto the ground and shook off a few signs. I could hear my teammates rooting me on in the background. I cocked my bat back and got ready. The first pitch he threw was a curve ball that caught the outside corner for a strike. "Beat me there," I thought. I stared down at the third base coach who gave me the "swing away" sign, I was ready again. The next pitch was straight heat just over the outside corner. I reached out for the fastball and crushed it to deep centerfield. The ball rose up quickly and I leaned forward, trying to coax it out of the park. Does it have enough? Does it have enough? I tried to move my feet and run toward first base, but I was frozen, captivated by the flight of the ball. I could see the center fielder running toward the wall, timing his jump. It's going, it's going, and then I felt a gust of wind at my back, the center fielder leaped, but it's...it's...gone! A homerun! Homerun, Jimmy Hanks. San Diego wins the World Series!

I trotted around the bases slowly, wading through the crowds of imaginary people who had mobbed the field. I crossed home plate, and sat down. Instantly, I was all alone. The dream was over and I was back in my scrubby jeans and SDU hat. The field was once again dead silent. When I drove home that night, I knew exactly where I was going. Back to SDU for my senior season.

I spent the next couple of days surfing with my brothers, until a phone call from Coach Tollberg convinced me to trade in my wet suit for a baseball uniform. He wanted me to play summer ball in Cape Cod, Massachusetts. This was the Rolls Royce of collegiate summer leagues and an opportunity I couldn't refuse. I packed up my stuff and boarded a flight to the Cape that night. Baseball had called, and I had answered.

In Cape Cod, against the best pitching that college baseball had to offer, I batted .298. I had played very well defensively that summer, and many scouts told me they were interested in drafting me. Again, I heard that I would be a top-ten round draft pick after my senior year. Only this time, I knew better than to listen. I believed that if I invested nothing in their lofty predictions of my draft status, then I wouldn't be devastated when I was back on my surfboard next summer, without a spot on a Minor League team. My new goal was just to enjoy the ride of being a senior in college. I had no idea it would turn out to be the ride of my life.

I knew that our team was going to be good that year, but I didn't know how good. Seth Ennis turned down a contract offer from St. Louis so he could direct our run at a Championship. His return meant that our pitching staff had an ace. Eli Menson, who recently reached the Majors in Cincinnati, was our catcher. He supplied Major League power in the middle of our line-up. All the guys who I had spent my entire college careers with, returned with their eyes on the ultimate prize, a Championship. Through it all, the glue that kept us together was Coach Jessup. As we made predictions of a banner season, he kept telling us to stop yapping and play.

The 1998 Sharks had everything. Pitching, defense, power, speed, and hitting. But still, I knew how many miles we'd have to travel to reach Topeka. We couldn't afford to get ahead of ourselves, or the dream of returning that dirt would be over.

The night before the first game of my senior season, I took out the envelope that I had placed the dirt in, and opened it up. I put my finger inside and felt around. I really wanted to get back to Topeka. We had a chance, I thought, a definite chance.

Chapter 11: "The Promised Land"

I peeked my head out from beneath the covers and waited for one of the men to turn and face me. They were in the middle of their conversation and hadn't bothered to notice my head sticking out again. I was sure that they would have some type of nasty reaction to my insubordination.

My ribs were starting to hurt from my body weight pushing down on them. I tried to readjust myself as stealthily as I could, attempting to take some pressure off my mid-section. I could only manage to crack my back. The sound was gruesome. I guess the men didn't hear the noise because they continued to discuss their plan to kill us in short whispers.

I started to imagine what they looked like beneath their masks. I pictured them both as young men, like myself. I was sure they had big dreams that they chased as well. I wondered what had happened in their lives that led them into this room, toting handguns and wearing masks.

It's strange the roads people take in life. My road has had bumps and steep hills along it, but I imagined these two men had run into many more obstacles along their way. I felt bad for them. They never got to experience just how great life can be. Maybe all the roads they'd traveled on turned out to be dead ends. I wanted to talk to them for a minute. I wanted them to know that dreams do come true. I remember when mine did...

As the regular season of my senior year came to a close, the focus of our team shifted toward the playoffs. We had won ten of our final twelve games, and that exclamation point on an already fine regular season earned us a number one seed in the East Regional. A ticket to Topeka would be on the line in Durham, North Carolina.

In the opening game, Seth Ennis lived up to his billing as one of the best college pitchers in all the land. He silenced the bats of Hamlitt University, and our line-up continued a torrid month of hitting. We'd opened up the playoffs with a 10-3 victory. Our momentum ebbed, though, when Virginia Southern pounded us, 14-4 in the next game.

This loss brought back some bad memories. After being eliminated the last two seasons in the regional, I couldn't help but think, "Here we go again." One more loss and our season would be over, my career would be done, and my promise of reaching Topeka would be broken. In order to advance from the loser's bracket, we would have to win three games on the same day. That task seemed daunting.

Our first assignment was the Durham Dogs, who would be playing in front of their rabid home fans. The Dogs' faithful came out in full force, but our bats made the most noise on that morning. The 8-5 victory put us in the finals against Birmingham, who had not yet lost in the double-elimination tournament. We'd have to beat them twice in a row to advance.

We staved off elimination in the afternoon game with a 3-2 win, which forced a final and decisive nightcap.

As the sun faded into the horizon, all of us grabbed some fruit from the snack bar and quickly gathered back in the dugout. We were not about to leave each other's side. We practiced, lived, ate, and traveled together every day. And now that the bus rides and plane trips were over, all we were left with was the hope that we would be able to win one game for the right to go to Topeka. That game was upon us.

The East Regional final against the Birmingham Generals was the best college baseball game I have ever played in. When such a high level of baseball is combined with the heightened sense of urgency that comes along with an elimination game, a great game becomes a classic one.

Birmingham took an early 1-0 lead with a home run in the bottom of the first. A half an inning later we were slapping hands in our dugout, after regaining the advantage. Before we could catch our breaths, Birmingham struck back. Just like that, we were down again, 3-2. By the time this "tug of war" match-up reached the bottom of the ninth, we had regained the lead at 4-3. The stadium was in a frenzy when Birmingham came to the plate.

They had a runner on third base with one out against our closer, Jack Kater, and with two chances to move him around, I began thinking about extra innings. Jack had other ideas. He promptly struck out the next batter, which left us one out away from Topeka.

The next guy up was a "dead-pull" left-handed hitter. Our infielders shifted to the right, to combat his tendency to hit the ball to that side of the field. As soon as the left-hander made contact with Jack's fastball, I thought that he'd found the only hole in the overcrowded right side of our infield. The pitch had been tattooed between Stan Davis and Will Russell, our middle infielders. Stan moved to his left, but had no chance to make the play. Will quickly shuffled to his right and went airborne to try and preserve our lead. The bouncing ball appeared to be way out of his reach. It hopped high above his head as he dove across the infield dirt. Will extended his five-foot-seven inch frame further than any of us could imagine, spearing the ball at the peak of its flight. In one of the most athletic movements that I'd ever seen, Will jumped up and threw a perfect strike to first base. His toss beat the runner to the bag by a hair! The umpire's out signal ended the game and kicked off our celebration.

I ran over to Will and tackled him. The two of us became the bottom of a growing "dog-pile." Soon, we were crushed by our teammates. We didn't care much though, we were headed to Topeka for the College Championship Series.

The next morning we left on a flight back to San Diego with "East Regional Champions" hats and t-shirts tucked away in our suitcases. They would be saved for some other time. For now, our focus had shifted to Topeka.

We arrived in Topeka three days after our return trip to San Diego. Our first opponent was Louisiana College and their infamous "gorilla ball." This term defined their ability to hit home run after home run. Louisiana College was advertised as the team of the 1990s, and SDU was billed as the team of the century. The first game of the College Championship Series would be a clash of the Titans.

Coach Jessup finished a short motivational speech prior to the game and we were ready to start. I put on my glove, fixed my hat, and stepped out of the dugout with a kick to my step. I glanced around at the television cameras, the huge stadium, and the twenty thousand screaming fans.

I got the chills as I approached the infield dirt. I was about to hop into position at third base, but instead I stopped and stared down at the chalked line in front of the bag. I was finally going to cross that line as a player. But there was something I had to do first. I reached into my back pocket and pulled out my envelope. As I bent over and emptied the dirt back onto the field, I felt something magical about the whole thing. I had made good on my promise to return the borrowed earth. I moved the dirt back and forth with my cleat, mixing the old with the new, until the brown blended together. Then I smiled as I touched third base. I had tears in my eyes. I punched the center of my mitt. "Let's go Jimmy, time to play some gorilla ball."

As it turned out, "gorilla ball" was simply too much for us that day. Louisiana College lived up to their reputation and blasted seven home runs to beat us, 11-10. Again, we had lost our first game in a double elimination tournament. Only this time we faced the difficult challenge of having to win five consecutive games against the nation's best.

In the first elimination game, we nipped the University of New York, 8-7 in an eleven-inning marathon. The victory over the nation's number one ranked team meant that we would have a full day of rest before our next game against River College.

My short break was hardly a relaxing one. Not only would I have to prepare for another elimination game, but the first day of the 1998 Major League baseball draft began that morning. A full year had passed since I had gone undrafted, and the memories of that day still haunted me. As the first day of selections drew longer and longer, I had still not been chosen. The same sick feeling I had a year ago was conjured up inside of me. Only this time the pain was sharper. After all, this was my last shot at getting drafted.

I had been sitting close to the phone in my hotel room from the moment I woke up that morning. Still, no one called. And yet again, I was left asking myself questions that I had no answers to. Where would I be going? In what round? Would I even be picked? I thought that maybe the team that selected me didn't know which hotel I was staying in, or maybe they wanted to tell me after our game. I was running low on excuses.

I had to kill some time so I played cards with my roommate, Will Russell, a fellow senior who was expecting a similar phone call from a Major League team. We played until we had to leave for lunch at 12:30 p.m. I hoped that when I returned to the room, the message light would be lit, and I would be a part of a Major League franchise. I desperately wanted the torture to be over.

When Will and I arrived back in our hotel room, we saw that the message light was not flashing. The torment continued, and as the time neared for us to go to the ballpark, I began to think that I'd been overlooked once again. I pulled up my left stirrup and got ready for what could have been the last game of my baseball career. Will was in the shower, and I was alone with my thoughts. SportsCenter was on in the background and Dan Patrick reminded me that our game would be televised on ESPN 2 in three hours. I walked over to the TV and clicked it off.

I could only hear the distant sound of water running in the bathroom and as I bent down to yank on my other stirrup, the phone rang. I turned around and stared at it nervously, wanting to move, but scared the call wasn't for me. It rang again. Finally, I jumped up and lunged for the receiver.

"Hello," I must have shouted.

"Hey, Jim, this is Doug Deaver from the Dallas Lonestars." I knew who Doug was. We'd spoken a few times.

"Hey Doug, how's it going?" This could be the call.

"Great, it's going great. You ready for your game tonight?"

"Already got my stirrups on." Although normally "small talk" didn't bother me, I really wanted him to get to the point.

"Well, I have some good news for you. We just picked you in the ninth round of today's draft. Congratulations, Jim, you're a member of the Dallas Lonestars franchise."

I pumped my fist in the air and tried to regain my breath. I managed to calm myself enough to speak. "Thank you so much, Doug. I've been waiting for this phone call for a long, long, time. You made a dream come true today. I guarantee that you won't be sorry you drafted me." I paused. "The Dallas Lonestars, huh? I like the Lonestars."

Dallas believed in me enough to make me a top ten round selection. I would have a chance to play Minor League Baseball after all. I felt like I had just won the lottery. But in reality, I knew I hadn't received this call by chance. Although I wasn't always the best athlete, I was usually the hardest worker. Getting drafted was my reward.

On the bus ride over to the field, I told a few guys about my selection. I didn't want to make a big deal about it. We had to focus on the task at hand, River College. We arrived at the stadium with a sense of purpose and so did our pitcher, Ralph Held. The freshman's stellar performance, in which he struck out 14 batters, was good enough for an 8-1 victory.

We were only three victories away from the Championship, but first we faced the nearly impossible task of defeating the Louisiana College Crawfish twice in a row. If our dream was going to continue, our pitchers would have to find some way to keep the ball in the park. Though we too could put up runs, there was no way we could match the "gorilla ball" tactics of Louisiana. We would have to win with our pitching. I guess someone told that to Seth Ennis because our ace limited the Crawfish to only four runs in our 6-4 victory.

We returned to play Louisiana the next night and our starting pitcher Mike Bender was just as dominant. He didn't back down from the Crawfish hitters. Instead, he busted his fastball inside on their hands, and one big bat after another barely mustered weak ground balls to our infielders. An 8-3 victory over Louisiana put us in the championship game against the Santa Fe University Desert. One game would decide which team would be the 1998 National Champions.

Santa Fe threw their best pitcher against us, a left-hander named Roy Gibbs. His arsenal included a nasty curveball that complimented his ninety-mile per hour fastball. Roy was the third pick in the first round of the draft a few days earlier and we congratulated him by scoring five runs in the top of the first inning, and three more in the second to take a commanding 8-0 lead.

The title was within our grasp and I think we all shifted into cruise control. In the dugout, we began to count the outs until a championship. We should have been counting the seconds until Santa Fe woke up. In the delirium of a possible blowout, we temporarily lost sight of our goal, and Santa Fe took advantage, scoring ten runs in the next five innings.

When the game entered the top of the seventh, our lead had been trimmed down to 13-10. A three run advantage was hardly safe in a game where the scoreboard was being lit up like the night sky on Independence Day. We needed some insurance runs. I was the leadoff hitter in our half of the seventh, I had to be the catalyst. I did my job, and scorched a single to left. Shortly thereafter, I was standing on third with two outs, and the bases loaded behind me. This was our chance to put on our own fireworks display.

Will Russell, our hottest hitter, was at the plate. He had already pounded four hits in his first four at-bats. One more big hit and he could put this one out of reach. On the first pitch to Will, I tried to distract Chip Williams, Santa Fe's relief pitcher, by charging down the third base line. Not only was he not distracted, he never even looked in my direction. At a crucial stage in the game, I knew that Williams had to be concerned with the batter, not my antics. On the next two pitches, I tried to disrupt him by bluffing a steal of home. Still, he remained focused, and had Russell pinned up against the wall with a 1-2 count.

Before the next pitch, I looked over at Coach Jessup in the dugout. The sun was in my eyes and I thought I saw him touch the tip of his hat and then wipe his hands down his thighs, the steal sign. That's impossible. How could he be giving me the steal sign? I shrugged my shoulders slightly, wanting him to repeat the signal. I must have been mistaken. There it was again. He touched the tip of his hat and then wiped his hands down his thighs. "Now let me get this straight," I thought. "Coach wants me to steal home with two outs, two strikes, and the bases loaded, with our hottest hitter at the plate, in the seventh inning of the College Championship Game?" Coach nodded his head and clapped his hands, making sure that I was on board with his plan. I tipped my helmet to him and nodded. I had to be ready.

As soon as Coach Jessup gave me the sign, my palms were suddenly soaked with perspiration. "Just get a good jump and be fast," I kept thinking to myself as I tried to relax and find oxygen. I took a few steps off third base and in my most focused of moments, I could no longer hear the twenty-thousand fans whose noise had been deafening all week long. The time seemed to move in slow motion. It was just Williams and me. My job was to beat his pitch to the plate, ninety feet away. If I was safe, I would give our team the momentum that we had lost, and our three run cushion would become a four run advantage. If I was out, I would kill our rally and such a costly mistake could inspire Santa Fe to make a dramatic comeback.

I increased my lead to about six steps off the bag and watched the pitcher as carefully as I could. Again, Williams didn't look in my direction, so I extended my lead a few more feet. I was waiting for him to pull off the rubber and throw over to third base. I was also anticipating the beginning of his windup. Either way, on his first movement, I would start my sprint toward home plate. The instant he started his windup I was off. I put my head down and motored as fast as I could. Williams noticed me taking off, and rushed his delivery to the plate. By the time I was half way down the line, I was sure I'd be a dead duck. I neared home, and looked up, angling my slide. Just as the ball arrived at the plate, so did I. I wasn't sure if I had beaten the tag, or if the tag had beaten me. The umpire would have the final say. I stared up through a cloud of dust to see the umpire waving the safe sign over and over again. "Safe! Safe! Safe!" he shouted into the Topeka sky. I had stolen home plate!

I usually show very little emotion on the field, but this time, I couldn't hold back. The sheer improbability of that moment gave me enough reason to celebrate. I tumbled out of my slide and started pumping my fists in a downward motion. I looked up and saw the entire team running off the bench to congratulate me. The guys grabbed me and started pounding on my helmet until I couldn't see straight. We had a 14-10 lead and we all knew that we were back in control.

After the celebration had subsided, Bryan Vogelsong, "the king of stats," approached me with a surprise. "You did it, man, 30-30. The first man in Sharks history." I'd become so wrapped up in trying to steal home, that I had forgotten my next stolen base was my 30th. When I "shagged" home, I became the first Shark ever to steal thirty bases and hit thirty home runs in the same season.

Before I could catch my breath and get a drink of water, Will promptly stung the ensuing pitch to right centerfield. His single knocked in two runs and gave us a commanding 16-10 lead. This base hit effectively ended the game. We went on to win by a football-like tally of 21-14.

For twenty-five guys and six coaches, there was no greater

sight in the world than seeing Jack Kater strike out that final batter. We mobbed the field as champions. In the midst of the pile on the pitcher's mound, I spotted Bryan Volgelsong and hugged him as hard as I could. Now, I had a stat for him. "The 1998 San Diego University Sharks are Champions. Put that one in your stat book, Bry, and don't ever forget it."

Chapter 12: "Baseball, Without the Perks"

I mumbled into the back of the tape as I glanced around the room in between the cracks in the brown blanket that covered me, "God, can you hear me? I'm waiting for the end to come now. Can you hear me?" One of the men was walking toward me and he looked me right in the eyes. I continued, "I'm ready if you need me, God." I thought those could have been my last words.

The man yelled at me, "I thought I told you to shut up!" He pushed my head down again. "I'm running the show here, not you."

My head popped out of the blanket and I stared directly at the gunman. He turned to face his partner, "That's it. This guy goes down first."

That guy was me. I was about to be shot and killed. The man walked toward me and loomed overhead like a rain cloud. In his fury, he yanked the brown blanket from on top of me. He raised his gun from his side and pointed it directly at my heaving body. I breathed deeply, ready for the end to come. My heart pounded harder than it ever had before and I made sure to keep staring directly into the man's eyes. He'd remember me. My final stare would make certain of that.

Knowing you're about to die is a strange experience. I felt as if I had to say some last words but the layers of tape had left my lips paralyzed. I mumbled as loud as I could, hoping that my words would be heard before I was shot.

"You have something to say?" the man asked harshly. "Go ahead tough guy." He bent down and ripped the tape away from my mouth, "Let's hear it."

Just as I started to speak, the front door came crashing into the living room. The police had smashed through and about ten charging cops bombarded the two gunmen. The criminals put up little resistance to the surprise attack. The man who held me at gunpoint knew he was outmatched and dropped his gun in an instant. His partner did the same. The police handcuffed both robbers and pinned them to the floor. They had now assumed our positions. We lay next to them on the floor as the police came around, untying us one by one. But I grew impatient as I waited for their help.

I pushed and pulled as hard as I could until I had freed myself from my restraints. The feeling of movement after such a long period of stillness was one that I would not soon forget. I moved around the room clumsily, like I was a toddler learning to walk for the first time. I think a part of me wanted to cry and another part of me wanted to celebrate.

"I'm out." I said joyfully.

I looked around the room and saw the cops helping Chad and Leon break away from their restraints. I walked over to my long time friend, Nick Erickson. I was still shaking and a tear rolled down my cheek. I was free.

I helped Nick separate his hands and then I ripped a piece of tape from his mouth.

He looked up at me with tears in his eyes, he was sweating profusely and his lips were purplish-blue. "Hey Jimmy, can you believe this?"...

Our bus started its engine in the 5:00 a.m. darkness of Auburn, New York. Nick was tapping me on the shoulder. "Hey Jimmy, can you believe this?" He was sitting next to me on my first Minor League bus trip. Nick was a fifteenth round selection of the Lonestars in the 1998 draft. Once again, we were teammates.

"It's crazy. Here we are, a couple of pro ballplayers, riding a bus to Montpelier, Vermont, going after the same dreams we talked about in high school. You know I was - "

I cut him off. I had heard this routine before. "I know, you were the first person to tell me that I was a ballplayer."

"Well I was." Nick smiled. He was wide awake, and got up to introduce himself to a few of the guys as they boarded the bus. The morning darkness and the dampness in the air made the impending trip to Vermont a little eerie. I knew that the choices I'd made that led me to that place, on that morning, were now final. My life as a professional baseball player was about to begin. As I settled into my seat, I watched our bus driver eat a bacon, egg and cheese sandwich in about three seconds. I could hear him attack his food. In the midst of devouring his breakfast, the man noticed me staring at him. He glanced back at me with butter dripping off of his double chin, "Welcome to Minor League Baseball, son." He swallowed loudly and I looked away, grinning.

I was real tired that morning. Waking up early had never been one of my favorite activities, and eight hour bus rides starting at 5:00 a.m. sounded about as much fun as kayaking down

Niagara Falls. At least Nick was there with me. He sat back down in the seat next to me as I zoned out, thinking about life at home. I thought about all the guys I knew who had just graduated. They would begin careers in banking, medicine, and finance. I wondered what their first day of work would be like. This was mine. I was sitting on a damp bus, watching our driver slobber all over himself while I was introduced to guys that I would play with and compete against, in order to achieve my dream of playing Major League Baseball.

Nick was talking again, "I can't believe you beat me in my last college game." I laughed at his comment, though I did feel for Nick. He was an outfielder for the University of New York, a team we eliminated with a miraculous 11-10 victory on our way to the national title. He continued, "Then you win the College Championship, and three days later, the two of us are sitting on a bus at the crack of dawn, headed to God knows where. Baseball's a funny game, huh? You start playing, and soon, it means everything to you. The friends you meet along the way are the same guys you pass going around the bases, or they're the ones sitting next to you on a bus ride to Vermont. It's awesome, you know?"

"Yeah it really is." I felt like I was back in high school again as I listened to Nick talk my ear off. But I didn't dare stop him. He was in a great mood and I guess I was too. I gave him a knuckle-bump and leaned my head against the window, hoping that I could catch up on some sleep.

In the span of just three days, I had gone from College Champion to a Minor League nobody, from a San Diego University Shark to an Auburn Beaver. But the part of the transition that really got me, was that someone was actually going to pay me to play baseball. My office would be the baseball field. My pen and pencil would be a ball and a bat, and if I had to do extra homework, I would go to the batting cage or field some grounders. Baseball was going to be my job. How could baseball ever be called a job? I would soon find out, the hard way.

The hard way means eight-hour bus trips and being thousands of miles away from home. It means living out of suitcases and learning how to sleep squeezed against the window of a shoddy bus. I learned about different cities and states that once seemed foreign to me. I remember thinking, on that first road trip, that the only thing I knew about Vermont was that there was a Ben and Jerry's factory somewhere. I just hoped that it was close to the ballpark.

When I was at SDU, I was only about a half-hour drive from a family dinner, or a chance to hit golf balls with my brothers. Those days were over. I had been assigned to Auburn, New York, the home of the lowest rookie ball affiliate of the Dallas Lonestars. I would be spending the season playing in the East Coast League, where the fans are sparse, and the travel seems never-ending. We made weekly road-trips to New York, Massachusetts, Pennsylvania and Vermont. Shuttling in and out of hotels and buses became a way of life. This was what Minor League Baseball *really* was, baseball without the perks.

I was having a hard time falling asleep on that first road trip. I moved around in my seat, searching for a comfortable spot, but unable to find one. A moment later Coach Sam Goddfrey stood in front of the team and officially welcomed the new guys. "Fellas, I need to make an announcement before you fall asleep." He spoke with purpose. His tough demeanor and sense of authority let me know right away that he was a baseball man, through and through. He rubbed his black moustache and continued, "Today, we're welcoming some new guys to our club. If you gentlemen would please stand up."

I stood up along with Nick and a few other guys. We all tipped our hats or gave a small wave. Not that anyone cared, or even looked up. In the Minor Leagues, you never like to see more players added to your team. Guys have to look out for their next paycheck, and a new player means that someone else is after your roster spot. Plus, the rest of the guys were already two weeks into their season, and they looked like they could use some rest. We quietly sat back down.

"Fellas, I'll tell you the same thing I told the rest of these guys the day they arrived. Big dreams start small, and they start now. I don't care what you did as a kid, in high school, or in college, this is the first day of the rest of your life. One out of every ten guys on this bus will put on a Major League uniform, maybe fewer than that. The chances are slim and the road is long. I know. I've been in your seat as a player, and I never made it to the 'show.' I respect you all for trying, and all I ask is that you play as hard as you can every night. That's the truest test of who will survive out here and who won't."

I knew the odds were against me when I came to Auburn, but I wouldn't let that stop me from trying.

During the next two months, I traveled around the East Coast, playing baseball six days a week. I slept in roadside Motel 8's, and threw back McDonald's "extra value meals" three times daily. All the while, I was surprised at how much better I was getting by playing the game every day. I learned how to consistently recognize a slider. I could see a change-up from a mile away, and I was hitting the hard stuff better than ever. I learned to shake off bad days, and bad weeks. I had to. I was playing baseball day in and day out, and if I didn't have a positive attitude, I would stand no chance on the field.

Our Auburn team advanced to the playoffs. I desperately wanted to use those extra games as redemption for an average season. I was able to do just that. During those five games, I hit .600 and helped our team claim the East Coast League championship. For the second time in three months, I was a champion. I don't know if I was more excited about the title or the fact that the victory meant the end to a long season. Either way, it was a chance for me to go home and spend some time with my family.

I flew back to San Diego the first week of September, knowing that I would be heading back to Kissimmee, Florida in March for spring training. When I walked off the airplane, holding a dusty baseball bag, I saw Mom waiting for me with open arms and a wide smile. Her expression changed a little as I got closer. I had grown my hair out to my shoulders, and I had a thick moustache to boot. The fast food had ballooned me up to two hundred thirty-five pounds. I think I actually scared her. I went to hug Mom and she kept touching my hair and looking at me as if to say, "What happened?" I think she liked my California look better than the hefty Minor Leaguer who came off the plane. I had been playing baseball for ten straight months, so I was anxious to spend some time away from the game. But I quickly found out that staying away wasn't an option. I couldn't help myself. I ended up going down to SDU everyday to work out with the team. I guess there are no days off when you love something so much.

Before I could catch my breath, my six-month "break" was over, and I returned to Florida for spring training. I arrived in Kissimmee in March, looking much different than the hairball that Mom picked up at the airport. I also trimmed off the extra weight I was carrying. Despite being in great shape, I soon learned that nothing could have prepared me for the torture of spring training.

That first spring was less about baseball, and more about survival. I would wake up at 6:15 a.m., run the obstacle course three times, do an abdominal workout, and run two miles, all before breakfast. After breakfast, I would field ground balls at third base. Then I moved on to batting practice. Batting practice is everybody's favorite time. We'd laugh, chat, and take huge rips at the ball, seeing who could hit the longest homerun. Finally, in the afternoon, we would play a nine-inning game. And at the end of the day, when most of the guys went back to the hotel, I would stick around the field to practice, just like I did in high school.

Baseball was my meal ticket and I was determined to make something of my time in camp. The extra practice paid immediate dividends when I was assigned to play class-A ball in Kissimmee. I had been moved up from rookie ball to high Single-A, which meant that I had skipped the Mid-Western League. This was a good sign. I knew that future Major Leaguers would have to bypass levels to reach the "show" in the prime of their careers.

Opportunities seemed boundless once I received that promotion. I only had to survive Kissimmee (Single-A Ball), Amarillo (Double-A Ball) and Cedar Rapids (Triple-A Ball), before I reached Dallas.

Kissimmee was a huge jump up from rookie ball. The players were much better at the Single-A level. Needless to say, I struggled early on. I guess slow starts are a fact of my baseball life, because I was awful at the beginning of my first full minor league season. When the first half ended, my average was a disgraceful .193.

I was having a very hard time playing in the Florida League, for a variety of reasons. Beyond the fact that I was facing the toughest pitching I had ever seen, I was doing so in front of about twenty-five people per game. As far as fan support was concerned, I had played in front of three times as many spectators in youth baseball as a kid. The Florida League is Minor League Baseball's version of being stranded on a desert island. The utter silence at these games would have made your local library sound like a rock concert.

On certain occasions, I would be able hear players on other teams having private conversations in the dugout. I even found myself overhearing fans in the stands, when they actually showed up. I realized once and for all, that baseball is only as good as its fans. And in Kissimmee, we didn't have any.

In the second half of the season, though, things started to turn around. I got used to empty stadiums, 110-degree heat, and some of the best pitching in the minors. I hit .288 with 13 home runs during the last seventy games. And for the second straight year, I saved my best performance for the playoffs. I batted .550 in the post-season and we won the Florida League. For the third consecutive season, I was a champion.

I felt strong, and completely focused when I returned to Kissimmee the next season for my second spring training. Upon arrival in Florida, executives in the Lonestars organization informed me that I would be playing for a chance to move up to Double-A. Although I was progressing quickly through the Dallas farm system, I knew the move to Amarillo would be the most important step on my road to the Majors. Double-A would mean that I was a legitimate Major League prospect. The Lonestars could afford to have some guys in A ball that were going nowhere in the game, but in Double-A, everyone was thinking about the "bigs." By plain percentages alone, my chances of becoming a Major Leaguer would increase dramatically with a promotion to Amarillo. Only ten percent of Single-A ballplayers reach the Majors, that number increases all the way up to thirty-three percent at the Double-A level. I knew I had to move quickly. I was racing against time, against age.

Spring training went great. I thought I had reinvented myself as a more polished version of the Jimmy Hanks that the Lonestars had seen in years prior. A few days before camp broke, I would find out if anyone had taken notice. "Assignment day" was upon us...

...I ran in place, kicking up small chunks of dirt from beneath the grass like a human lawn mower. I wanted to keep my feet moving to fight the morning chill of central Florida. I couldn't play with frozen feet, not today. I looked down at my beat up size twelve cleats. They looked especially worn out next to the bright green grass of the baseball diamond and the true brown of the infield dirt. I promised myself that if I made the jump to Double-A ball, I'd buy a new pair. That morning, I would find out whether or not I'd be able to afford them.

"Assignment day" is the day that each player is assigned to a particular Minor League team, or told to go straight home. I'd been awake since 5:00 a.m., wondering where I would be playing in the upcoming season. Every year three days before spring training ends, Minor Leaguers around the country can count on the most nerve-racking hours of their season.

Cold sweat dripped from my forehead onto the soft green grass of Kissimmee, Florida. I was twenty-four years old, and if I wanted to have a legitimate chance of playing Major League Baseball, I couldn't afford to spend another season in Single-A. This spring training marked the start of my second full season in the Minor Leagues. I had to keep moving up. If I stood still for too long, I would need to find a new profession. I ran faster, kicking up bigger and bigger chunks of dirt. I was excited. In a few hours, I would find out my baseball destiny....

And that's where this whole story starts. On "assignment day," in Kissimmee. The day my life turned upside down. The day I became a Major League prospect and stared death directly in the face. I'd made the jump to Double-A, Amarillo. I was supposed to be celebrating that night. Instead, the 16th day of March, in the year 2000, turned into my worst nightmare. I thought no one would ever be able to hear this story. I was sure that I was going to die.

Chapter 13: "The Show"

We were all a part of a cops and robbers movie and the good guys had prevailed. As a few police cars left the scene with our captors handcuffed in the back seat, our five faces were glued to the window, watching the end of this drama unfold. A short stocky police officer approached us from behind. He was walking beside the pizza delivery guy who we'd seen a half-hour earlier. The officer spoke loudly, "You guys should thank your lucky stars you ordered pizza from this guy." He guided the bashful teenager toward us. "He called us up and told us to check this place out. The kid's a real hero."

I looked over at the teenager. He stood about five feet eight inches tall, was covered with pimples, and couldn't have weighed more than a hundred- fifty pounds. He looked awkward, the way I looked when I was sixteen. I shook his hand as if he were the President of the United States. We all did. One by one we thanked him with all our hearts for saving our lives. He was blushing and a little embarrassed. "It was no problem," he uttered with a small grin.

I put my arm on his shoulder, "I guess you understood what I was trying to tell you at the door."

The boy spoke, "I saw you mouth the word 'help', so I figured the best thing I could do was make believe I didn't see you, and call the police."

A short woman holding a camera walked into the room and took a photograph of the five of us and the pizza delivery boy. She told us that we would be front- page news in

Kissimmee the next morning. The officer escorted the delivery boy out the door, but before the kid left he turned to face us. "Can you guys do me a favor?"

"Anything you want, kid," Leon Thompson smiled as he spoke.

"Hold on one second," the boy said as he raced out the front door toward his car. We all looked at each other curiously. A moment later he was back holding a baseball and a magic marker. "I've been coming down to the field every day after school since spring training started. I recognized your faces and I was wondering if you guys would sign this for me? I'm a huge baseball fan. I play for Kissimmee High, third base. I'm going to play in the Majors someday."

Now I was smiling from ear to ear, "Me too, buddy." We all chuckled as the ball was passed around to each one of us. We had something in common, all six of us shared the same dreams. I spoke to the boy just before I signed his ball, "I'd be proud to be your teammate."

I had survived the scariest night of my life and looked forward to a bright future. On the other hand, the two gunmen would be spending much of the rest of their lives in prison.

To this day I'm still in shock about what transpired in Kissimmee. I have come to truly appreciate the gift of life, we all should, because the show might be over tomorrow...

The medicine I took to overcome the horror of that situation was baseball. Three days after the holdup, I was headed to Amarillo, my new baseball home. I soon realized there was no experience like a Minor League game in Amarillo. I loved the energy that their lively crowd gave off when a play I made fired them up. I could feel the electricity in the air after a standing ovation and as the fans sat back down, I could almost hear the grumbling of fathers and sons talking baseball. Night after night, the fans at Amarillo Stadium did their best to make us feel like we were already Major Leaguers.

During my Double-A season in Amarillo, I batted .325 with 33 homeruns and 104 RBI's in 140 games. All three totals were career high marks for me. I think I even surprised myself. Everything went perfectly during the regular season, and we qualified for the playoffs.

After surviving a best of five series with Reno that went the distance, we would play Ames, Iowa for the League Championship. Behind a dominant cast of starting pitchers, we took a strangle hold on the series with a three game to one advantage. Ames would have to beat us three times in a row in front of our energized home crowd. Ten thousand screaming fans, the largest crowd of the year, packed Amarillo Stadium in anticipation of seeing their team celebrate a League Championship.

Ames took a 3-1 lead in the fourth inning and just as the celebration looked like it would have to be put on hold for another night, we rallied behind the bat of Chad Barnett to take a 5-3 lead in the fifth. Kevin Cove added a home run, giving us a three run cushion going into the ninth. Amarillo Stadium erupted in a sea of celebration when Hector Gomez pumped a fastball by Ames' Mark Tontz, ending the game. I hugged Chad Barnett and Kevin Cove, two guys who had survived that fateful night in Florida with me. For the three of us, our road wasn't just from A ball to Double-A. In between, we almost lost everything.

All of the guys stood together behind the pitcher's mound as our coach John Kingman was presented with the League Championship trophy. Coach Kingman grabbed the microphone and thanked the fans for their season-long support.

We all applauded once Coach had finished, and began exiting the field. Another year of Minor League baseball had come to a close, and while I was elated about our championship, I faced the fact that my Major League time clock was ticking rapidly.

The applause came to a halt as Coach Kingman spoke again, "I can't wait to do this all over again next year." The crowd went into an uproar, and all the guys stopped before leaving the field. Coach went on, "Well, before we call it a night and say goodbye for the winter, I have one last announcement that I want to make. Jimmy Hanks, get over here," Coach demanded with a huge smile on his face.

As I moved towards the front of the pitcher's mound where Coach was standing, I became very nervous. My heart pounded rapidly. What was Coach doing? I had a strong regular season, so maybe he was going to acknowledge me in front of the crowd. I was uncomfortable with such a notion. The entire team should be recognized, not just me.

Coach looked at me and spoke. "This morning I received a call from the General Manager of the Dallas Lonestars, Jake Minnis. He had some super news for you. I wanted to tell you earlier but I was waiting for the right time." The crowd pumped in some more noise. "This sure feels like the right time, Jimmy."

No way, I thought, there was no chance, it was just not

possible that...

"You've been called up to the Major Leagues. The Dallas Lonestars. You leave tomorrow. I'm so proud of you, Jim. Good luck in 'the show' fella."

Right then, I lost control. I dropped down to my knees and started crying like I never had before. That was it for me, the epitome of everything I had worked for. I was a Major Leaguer. I had received a promotion from Double-A straight to the Majors, bypassing Triple-A in the process. When I finally regained my composure, Coach Kingman helped me off the ground and we embraced in a hug. Next stop, Dallas.

The flight to Dallas had me arriving in time for batting practice before a 7:00 p.m. game against Los Angeles. A small man, wearing a suit with a Dallas Lonestars logo embroidered onto the breast pocket, led me into Dallas' brand new Lonestar Park. He brought me into the depths of the stadium, and after walking through hallway after hallway, we finally made our way into the clubhouse.

After I picked my jaw up off the floor, I began to survey the room. I had never seen anything like this place. Everything was brand new. I mean everything. There was a huge television showing last night's highlights, with cushy leather couches sitting in front. There was a ping pong table, a sauna, a hot tub, and a buffet with enough food to serve every person who bought a ticket to see the game that night. I munched on a piece of delicious fried chicken. Even the food tasted better in the Majors.

"Hanks, your locker is over there," the tiny driver pointed to his left.

I walked over to my locker that looked more like a hotel

room. Three Lonestars jerseys hung next to one another. There was a gray one for warm ups, blue for road games, and white for home. Socks and pants were folded neatly beneath. I turned my white home jersey around, "Hanks" and the number thirty, were stenciled perfectly on the back. I laughed out loud. I was really here. There were three freshly carved bats, which were the exact weight and length that I used, waiting for me. Then, I glanced down at two pairs of size twelve cleats that sat alongside the lumber. In the Minors, I was always saving money for new cleats. Now I had two new pairs waiting for me, just my size.

I quickly changed into my warm up gear and sat down on the chair in front of my locker. I laced up my shiny black cleats and put on a Lonestar cap that fit perfectly. Then I grabbed a pair of bats, and ran down a never-ending tunnel.

When I emerged, I was standing on a Major League field, the most beautiful sight I had ever seen. As soon as I set foot onto perfectly manicured Lonestar Park, a baseball from the batting cage rolled in front of me. I bent down to pick it up and I couldn't believe my eyes. The ball was brand new. In the Minors, we'd reach into the trash to save a ball. Now I'd be hitting brand new ones in batting practice.

I approached the batting cage and saw real Major Leaguers pounding balls. After fifty consecutive lasers, I realized that these were the best hitters I'd ever seen. That's when it actually occurred to me that I was surrounded by the best players in the world. I recognized all the names on the backs of the jerseys. Some of the guys who I watched play the game as I grew up, were now standing next to me as teammates. It was a magical feeling.

As it turned out, I never got to take a cut in batting practice. After the National Anthem, I got comfortable on the bench and enjoyed the best seat I'd ever had for a Major League Baseball game. I made a couple of new friends, munched on sunflower seeds, and drank the coldest Power-Ade I had ever tasted. We all clapped and rooted for our team. I was just another guy on a Major League club.

As I threw another dozen seeds into my mouth in the bottom of the eighth inning, I heard a voice at the other end of the dugout.

"Hey, Hanks!" Lonestars' Manager Larry Diggs screamed to me.

"Yeah Coach?" I shouted back through a mouthful of seeds.

"Grab yourself a bat, kid! You're on deck."

TEST YOURSELF....ARE YOU A MAJOR LEAGUE READER?

(Visit www.scobre.com and send your answers to info@scobre.com to find out if you are a Major League reader. Please remember to leave us your e-mail address so we can send you your scores. Good luck!)

Chapter 1: "Up, Down or Out?"

Why was there an eerie feeling on "assignment day"?

What is "old trusty", and what memory did it conjure up inside of Jimmy's head?

What does the title of this chapter, "Up, Down, or Out?" refer to?

ESSAY

Gloating or celebrating your promotion in front of your fellow teammate is prohibited in Minor League Baseball. Why was this "etiquette" especially important on "assignment day"? What lesson did you learn from the etiquette of the ballplayers in this chapter?

Chapter 2: "A Tough Fall"

Who were the "Tidal Waves"?

Why was Coach Custis upset with Jimmy's first goal?

What did Coach Custis mean when he said "failure is the mother of all great success?"

ESSAY

Jimmy was cut from the "Tidal Waves," but his response to this adversity was to stand up and try again. Name a time in your life when you took a "tough fall" and stood back up and kept trying.

Chapter 3: "No Easy Way Out"

What was Jimmy most afraid of when he began to think about dying?

Why did Jimmy decide to peg Silvano?

Can you think of a time in your life when you refused to take the "easy way out?"

ESSAY

Jimmy was stereotyped as a "surfer kid" because of his hair and his Ocean Town background. Have you ever been stereotyped or stereotyped someone else? How did that make you feel? How did it make Jimmy feel?

Chapter 4: "The Umbrella Man"

What does Jimmy mean when he says, "A small victory for the good guys?"

According to Jimmy, what was his "greatest weapon" against Nick when they spoke about the possibility of being professional baseball players?

Who is the "umbrella man" and who did he work for?

ESSAY

In this chapter, we learn that Jimmy is planning his "Road to the Majors." What future aspiration do you have? What are you doing to ready yourself for that career?

Chapter 5: "Back on Track"

Why did Jimmy find inspiration in the life of Michael Jordan?

Why did Roger want to play basketball with Jimmy?

Why was the SDU letter so important to Jimmy?

ESSAY

In this chapter Jimmy is "Back on Track" with his goal of going to school at SDU. Do you have a college that you dream of attending? What steps will you take to make your college dreams come true?

Chapter 6: "Blaine Field"

How was "Big Boned" Lionel Strone tipping off his pitches?

Why did Jimmy originally feel inclined to play baseball at Pacific?

What made him change his mind about enrolling at Pacific?

ESSAY

The word "perseverance" is used throughout this book. How does Jimmy persevere on his road to SDU? Have you ever persevered? Explain.

Chapter 7: "Digging a Hole"

Why is this chapter entitled "Digging a Hole?"

What news did Jimmy receive when he went back to confront Coach Jessup about not being on the traveling roster to Hawaii?

Why were the fans in Hawaii laughing at Jimmy?

ESSAY

In Chapter 7, we read how Coach Jessup taught his players to bring "passion" to whatever they do in life. What does the word "passion" mean, and what does Coach mean when he says "if you have passion, you will reach the Majors in whatever you do in life?"

Chapter 8: "The Wrong Side of the Fence"

In this chapter, what does it mean to be on "the wrong side of the fence?"

Why did Jimmy refuse to step over the chalked lines at Rockport Stadium?

When Jimmy spoke with Coach Horn, why did he second-guess his decision to attend SDU?

ESSAY

In this chapter, Jimmy feels like he is part of the team, though, he is standing on "the wrong side of the fence."

Name a time when you felt like you were part of a team? How did you contribute to this team? How did your team exhibit teamwork?

Chapter 9: "It's Just a Game"

What turned Jimmy's plans of starting at third base upside down?

To break out of his terrible slump, Jimmy tried a number of things. Name at least two.

What are some things that Jimmy loves about baseball? Name at least two.

ESSAY

Roger tells Jimmy to play baseball like he did when he was a kid, and not to let the game turn into a business? How can baseball turn into a business? Mentally, what did Jimmy do to change his attitude?

Chapter 10: "Getting Up"

Why did Jimmy want to make sure he got his head out from beneath the blanket?

Why was Jimmy considering quitting the game of baseball?

Why did Jimmy have options beyond baseball?

ESSAY

In this chapter, Jimmy says, "I can take more punches than

you can." What does that mean? In what ways does he exhibit this sentiment throughout the book?

Chapter 11: "The Promised Land"

What is "gorilla ball" and which team used this tactic?

Why was Jimmy so surprised to get the steal sign from Coach Jessup?

Why did Jimmy pause before he crossed the chalked line at Rockport Stadium?

ESSAY

In Chapter 11, Jimmy was rewarded for his years of hard work when he was selected in the Major League Draft. What lesson does this teach you about hard work? How can you apply Jimmy's work ethic to your life?

Chapter 12: "Baseball, Without the Perks"

What does the title "Baseball, Without the Perks" refer to?

Beyond the tough pitching, what was another reason that Jimmy struggled early on in Kissimmee?

Why was Double-A considered such an important step toward the Major Leagues?

ESSAY

In this chapter, Jimmy says "that there are no days off when you love something so much." Is there something in your life that you can't stay away from because you love it so much? What are you passionate about?

Chapter 13: "The Show"

Why did Jimmy uncomfortable about being acknowledged in front of the Amarillo crowd?

Why was Jimmy so thrilled to have new cleats waiting for him in his locker in Dallas?

Why does Jimmy truly appreciate the gift of life these days?

ESSAY

Congratulations! You have completed your first Scobre Press book! Now tell us what you learned from Jimmy's life, and how you plan on making your own dreams come true.